This book is a work of nonfiction. Names, characters, places, and incidents either are products of the authors' imagination or are used fictitiously. Any resemblance to actual events, locals, or persons, living or dead, is entirely coincidental.

DON'T LOOK
LIKE WHAT I'VE
BEEN THROUGH
STACEY BARLOW

Don't Look Like What I've Been Through

By Stacey Barlow

Cover Illustrated by Darlene A. Taylor

Created by Jazzy Kitty Publications

Logo Design by Justin Ackerman

Editor: Anelda L. Attaway

ISBN 978-1-954425-24-8

Library of Congress Control Number: 2021907726

DEDICATIONS

I wish to dedicate this book to my cousin, my "ACE," who will forever be in my heart. I'm still missing you.

Angela K. Perry

{April 24, 1967 ~ December 5, 2011}

My dear sweet cousin, **Stephanie Gooden**, your life was not lived in vain. God has His angel back.

{Jul 10, 1976 ~ October 9, 2013}

Another precious jewel in my heart was taken away. My play partner and cousin, **Roland C. Harris**. You lived a GOOD life.

{October 18, 1921 ~ October 27, 2013}

The heartbeat that never stopped beating.

Thank you for being the affectionate one

Odis L. Jackson

{April 27, 1967 ~ -June 11, 2021}

ACKNOWLEDGMENTS

I am putting God first in all the things that I do. He is the head of my life and watches over me daily. If it had not been for the Lord on my side, I truly don't know where I would be. I thank Him for giving me a gift and the talent to write. God knows my heart and He also knows that writing is my passion. Through Him, one of my desires is to do what He will have me to do and that He will continue to show me favor through His grace and mercy.

I want to thank my publisher, Anelda Attaway, for believing in me and giving me a voice. Thank you for pushing me and giving me space and freedom to write what's inside.

My mentor, Ms. Abiola Abrams, for also believing in me and showing me that I can overcome any obstacle that stands in my way. Thank you for years of friendship and for bringing out the "goddess" that dwells within me. You are the most amazing woman that God has put on this earth. I am truly blessed to have you in my life.

Evangelist Stacy Lattisaw ~ Jackson may not know it, but you will know it now that God spoke through you and gave me something to build on because of what you said. I really appreciate you taking the time to speak to me and giving me permission to do what should have been done a very long time ago. May God continue to bless and carry you and your family to higher heights.

Tionne "T-Boz" Watkins, your kind words helped me realize that everyone won't play fair in this world. We need to be careful of who we associate ourselves with. I love you.

Peppur Triplett and DeeAnna Jonelle Smalls, the two most beautiful women ~ sister friends in my life who helped me keep my head above water. I love you.

Harold Whaley, the most influential man I've ever gotten to know these past few years. Your friendship means the world to me. Thank you for letting me in and inspiring me to be at my best. I love you.

Steve Harrison, the man with the plan whom I have learned much from over the years. You have been a central part of my life, enabling me to go forth with my goals and dreams. You have taken that fear of "not being the best" out of me and taught me how to put my best foot forward, and for that, I really appreciate it. God bless you.

Annie Jennings is the most professional agent of all times in my eyes. I appreciate you giving me an outlet to share with the world.

Rosalyn McMillan, for allowing me to use "bits and pieces," may God continue to bless and keep you. Thank you so very much.

My family, mother, grandmother, sister, brother-in-law, aunt, uncle-in-law, uncle, niece, and nephew, you are all the reason why I love you wholeheartedly. Thank you for your support.

My friends, who are too many to name, you should know who you are. Thank you for endless nights of conversation when I couldn't sleep.

Special thanks to Ms. Gina Haggard for your years of dedicated friendship. I love you.

EPHESIANS 1:16 CEASE NOT TO GIVE THANKS FOR YOU, MAKING MENTION OF YOU IN MY PRAYERS.

TABLE OF CONTENTS

INTRODUCTION

When life gives you sour grapes, make grape juice. Not everyone is born with a silver spoon in their mouth where everything is easy and handed to them on a silver platter. Even those in wealthy families have a hard time fitting in with a crowd unless they are around other wealthy individuals. Still, that crowd might not be as accepting as others. The author has a wonderful family and a mother who spoiled her but still taught her the value of a dollar. This book will allow the reader to walk the path of the author born with Cerebral Palsy. A disability that causes brain damage at birth. Life can be difficult growing up, but it can also be even harder having a disability.

In this book, I will show you how to overcome the obstacles of family life, school life, relationships outside of family and the end result of making dreams come true. Everybody has a different story to tell. You may have lived through something you can't get over. I'm here to tell you that there is hope for your future and a light at the end of the tunnel. I lived it and survived because of a higher power that I believe in.

There is always an upside to every situation you face. People will come in and go out of your life to teach lessons. It's up to you and only you to decide whether you will continue to remain destructive or let go and find the peace and happiness you deserve. If greater things happen to me, they can happen for you too.

This may be a chance of a lifetime to finally get rid of all the poison in your system. Get your tissues ready. Cry if you have to.

CHAPTER 1

Little Girl Lost

<u>Luke 19:10</u>: "For the Son of man is come to seek and to save that which was lost."

A child remembers much as he or she is growing up. What I remember at the age of four and what was said that happened at the age of three. At the age of three, I don't remember my great grandfather, my grandmother's dad. But I can tell that he was a very loving and caring individual. In my mind, from the stories being told, he was stern. I was told that I had climbed on his lap wanting to play, but he didn't feel like it. He might have played for a little while and got tired. "Get down baby, papa, don't feel like playing." And with those words, he left this world. It's wonderful though that we keep his memory alive by listening to stories of my grandmother growing up in the home that I grew up in. I remember going to this place I thought was a school filled with bright colors and a drab brown. That was at the time I thought a teacher, who was actually a psychiatrist, would call me into this bigger room and sit me down to talk. Not remembering what the discussion was about, I know she asked questions. I was four years old at the time. She was a goddess to me with long flowing brown hair, short, and wearing a brown bell bottom suit. It was the 70's, so this was the style. This place was for "challenged" children like myself who were blind, deaf, can't speak, or can't walk. It's now for senior citizens who can't do for themselves.

I remember taking the bus in the morning to go to the place. Maybe that's the reason I thought it was a school. I have memories of sitting up in town waiting on the bus or the bus waiting on me. I hated to leave my mother and go to a place where I felt alone. She was my protection. I can even remember the smell of the morning air and me being half asleep waiting for the bus. The first thing that I had to do was eat breakfast. It always seemed sunny out. I hated getting on the mat when it was my turn to get stretched, which was my therapy. It hurt. I didn't know why it hurt, but it did. During the time the therapist was stretching my legs, it seemed to take forever to stretch, and the pain level was an eight on the body scale. I think she deliberately tried to hurt me. Out of all the things I had to do there, that was the most fun. When it was time for me to do leg work, the assistant or whomever it was having to supervise the children would strap me down in this concoction of a wheelchair would tell me to pedal until my time was up. I would fall asleep EVERY TIME. What confused me was that when we didn't go to the specific place, there was another place that was always available for us to have some kind of fun or lessons. But wherever I went, I felt safe. There was this building that I went to; it seemed much smaller than the one I had been going to. The other children and I sat on the floor all bunched up together to watch a children's story. That children's story was "The Ugly Duckling" in the movie though I don't remember the duckling turning into a beautiful swan but that's how the story goes. Using the bathroom that day should not have been that difficult. I had on a dress. To make a long story short, I fell into the toilet, and my mother had to bring me some more clothes. That was truly embarrassing for me because I had to walk around with that urine smell on me. The teacher was nice enough to clean me up the best she could and nice enough to call my mother. Everything after that is a blur.

CHAPTER 2

Little Girl Found

Jeremiah 29:14: "I will be found by you," says the Lord. "I will end your captivity and restore your fortunes."

At eight years old, I remember having the Bible in my lap and I read this story about criticism. At least, that's what I call it. Jesus was asking, why are you worried about the beam in someone else's eye when you have one in your own eye? You can't help your friend with that beam when you can't see past your own. Get that beam out of your eye then you will be able to see well enough to help your friend. This was one of my favorite stories. There was this movie that I had seen and it was about this preacher claiming to be a healer. The show was in black and white. The preacher healed a blind man, but it seemed as though the people in the town didn't like him and killed him.

I enjoyed Sunday school because I had a wonderful teacher who knew her Bible well and she passed her knowledge on to us the best way she could. To her, I give her my love because she is who she is. I just dreaded getting up and going to church but when I stepped across the threshold of the church, I was fine ~ prepared to give praises to God in song. The choir was full of harmony, and even to us, we felt the spirit from hearing the harmony. We found that our best practice was on Saturday morning at 10:00 a.m. We played, laughed and prayed. Rehearsal went fast when it was done that way. When there was a "mess up," we would smile and keep on going because our piano director instilled in us to make a joyful noise unto the

Lord.

Growing up, I really didn't understand the meaning of who God should be to me and for me. I felt obligated to go to church because it was supposed to be good for me. Going to school, meeting friends, cutting up, doing work in class, and playing, I never gave it a second thought to God protecting me throughout the day; even though getting prepared for school, mother doing my hair and grandmother fixing breakfast every morning, He still watched over me and my family. During the school years, just like every child, I was teased. Now, it's called bullying. Back then, we would laugh and walk around in a circle as if we were going to fight but nothing ever jumped off. And the last words that were basically said, "I know you know who my mother is." My mother would always tell me she had my back and anything or anyone who bothered me she would have a discussion with his or her parents. Jr. High and High School were totally different. You are learning more for one thing, and the second thing would be the friends you had before; you may not have those friends in high school. From the 9th grade to graduation, it seemed easy. Or was it? For me, I made it look easy.

CHAPTER 3

Back Down Memory Lane

<u>Psalms 23:4</u>: "Yea though I walk through the valley of the shadow of death, I will fear no evil for thou art with me."

Okay, so my teenage years may have been just like any other teenager; we all go through the same things: pimples, boys or girls, homework, tests, trips, driving and of course...dating. I have had good friends to look out for me and my mother always knew who I was with. I came in on time too. I knew I was in good hands. Back in the day, we went to house parties where the parents chaperoned the more immature teenagers. I never did anything to embarrass the family name, but I was known for dancing like there was no tomorrow, but that wasn't enough. I was missing something. I had a loving family, a good education and wonderful friends to boot. I can only imagine what my life would have been like if I had lived with the man I call "invisible." {dad/father}. You know the ones who just spill their seed and hardly ever show his face? Yeah, that one.

I'm nowhere near as angry as I used to be 26 years ago when he denied that I was his child and I look just like the man. And with that revelation, it made me begin to wonder who I was if he wasn't the father. He became Peter to me...no, that's not his name. I am speaking about Peter in the Bible, where he denied Jesus three times. The first time he denied me, he was going around in my hometown, stating that I wasn't his; the second time was in the courtroom when the lawyer asked, "And with this union, there was a child?" His response was, "They say..." "They" meaning who? Wooooosaaaah, okay, the third and the final straw was when I called him to ask him did he say those things, and his response was "no," and an explanation. At that point, I didn't want to hear anything he had to say. I lost contact with him after that.

Let's back up to house parties and school. As I said, something was missing because the parties just weren't enough. I'm not talking about heavy drinking and drugs. I don't like to sneeze, so I don't see how anyone can put that white powder up their nose. Puts me in the mind of The Artist Formerly Known As Prince with his song "Pop Life" and the line he sings, "whatchu puttin' in your nose? Is that where all your money goes.?" I am blessed to not have that desire to crave that. There were other things that happened in my life that were just as bad. Being a child of the '70s, every child doesn't go through the same things. Remembering when I was five years old and spending the summer with my aunt Hazel in Galveston, TX. I fell asleep on the floor while watching television. I remember being lifted and taken to the bedroom. Later, I was awakened by a tall, slender young man whom I recognized as my cousin who might not have been.

He proceeded to stay in the room, turning on the radio and sliding under the covers next to me. I pretended to be asleep, but I stared out of the window, looking at the lamppost with a beige light. This "guy" continued to shake me to get my attention until I turned over to see what he wanted. "Let's play school," he said. And I responded, "I just got out of school. Why would I want to *play* school?" He retracted, "Okay, let's play house. You be the mommy and I'll be the daddy." I looked at him and said, "I'm not grown." I noticed this beautiful necklace around his neck, and I wanted to see it. I remembered it like it was yesterday. He said to me that he would let me see it if I played house with him. Being five, wanting things that I ask for without really knowing the consequences, I see now is a dangerous thing. He took the necklace off and let me wear it. He slid out of bed to turn the radio up. He slid back in the bed and told me to be quiet and lie still. He whispered in my ear, "This is what mommy and daddy's do when daddy comes in from a hard day's work." He unbuckled my jumpsuit, his pants and started rubbing up against me. My mind concentrated on the lamp post outside, dreaming of days I could run away and make something of myself while this song called "Rock The Boat" played in the background. He was hurting me and I started to cry. He called himself, trying to comfort me by telling me not to cry and wiping my tears. A few minutes later, I thought he had used the bathroom on me. He told me to lie still again, stating that he would be right back. He appeared again with a towel to wipe what I thought was urine off my clothes. He told me not to tell anyone, or he would come back and really hurt me. I found it strange that he would say that to me when he had told me earlier that it's what mommy's and daddy's do. Just to make sure that I wouldn't tell it, he wanted me to ride with him when the family left the house. By then, I was frightened of him. When the summer was over and I went home, I tried to tell the one family member I loved and trusted the most, but she didn't understand. I blocked that memory somehow until I was in my 30s and the radio station played the same song one night when I was sitting in the car with my mother and I asked her to turn the radio off. She asked me why and that was the beginning of a closer relationship.

CHAPTER 4

I Am Like You

<u>1 John 4:17</u>: "Herein is our love made perfect, that we may have boldness in the day of judgment: because as he is, so are we in this world."

Every child wants to be the apple of their parent's eye, do things that are pleasing in their sight and make them smile. I would tell anyone that I am not perfect and I don't claim to be. I wasn't born with a silver spoon in my mouth, nor did I become famous at 13. In some cases, people who strive to get where they are going don't make it until they get older. I dreamed of being on television and I still may get my chance, but God gave me a gift and a niche that is way better than being on television. This gift God gave helped me to express feelings, possibly the same feelings that others may go through or things that happened to them. After school in what is now called middle school, the kids that were waiting for their buses to come to take them home would all play a game. On this particular day, the kids decided to play freeze tag. One of my schoolmates was it and I ran to not get frozen. I shot behind the school building, where he caught me and threw me to the ground. Just like when I was five, it started all over again. He had gotten me dirty. I had on a white shirt that day with a gold flower on the front. I had to go home...dirty. I just told my mother I fell. Prior to that, I ran to the bathroom, trying to clean myself up. Another student came into the bathroom to ask me if I was okay. She told the teacher, the teacher told the principal and I was called into the office the following school day to relive the horrible incident.

The guy was suspended from school that day, but his friend got wind of it, cornered me by the lockers with a knife and said, "you got my friend suspended. Tell it on me and I'll kill you." I walked right back up to the principal's office and told him what happened and he was kicked out of school. By then, I got tired of being picked on and threatened. I had no other choice but to be bold so that no one else would have to go through what I went through. I continued to be molested for the next five years of my life by a family member. Quietly suffering in silence, he too said that if I told, he would kill me. Without even really thinking, I decided that since I'm being threatened all the time, I was going to beat them to the punch and do the job myself. I was over at my cousin's home one day and my mind started wandering because I was just feeling out of place, so I took a knife from the kitchen and locked myself in one of the bedrooms. As I began to cry, I held the knife to my wrist. Thinking nothing more but just to end it all, I pressed the point deep into my skin, not yet cutting but feeling the sting of the point. In an instant, the few that were there started banging on the door to let them in. I was thinking, *"goodness! Can I not die in peace?"* My elder cousin pushed his way through the door as my other cousin proceeded to take the knife from my hand. My older cousin called himself talking to me with encouragement but I didn't want to hear it.

Am I fascinated with death? Not really. When you have that stronghold of wanting to end it all, at that moment ~ nothing else matters. I wrote of death, but that doesn't make me suicidal, as some people would think. Many people have that thought crossed their minds. Some go through with it and die; others try and live. Those who live should know that it is NOT their time to leave this earth. God will call you when He's ready for you.

CHAPTER 5

What God Has For Me

<u>Esther 2:9</u>: "And the maiden pleased him, and she obtained kindness of him; and he speedily gave her things for purification, with such things as belonged to her, and seven maidens..."

In the book of Esther, the king showed Esther favor because she carried herself well and obeyed the king. Of course, the king had a queen who disobeyed him, so he put her away. Now, God made it so that this king would show Esther favor and eventually, she became queen. If we wait on God, ask in His name, and do as He says, He will show you favor. He shows everyone favor by giving each one a day of grace and mercy. We have all heard, *"what God has for me is for me."* I believe that and I am working toward that goal of achieving what belongs to me. It all started when I was a little girl, as previously stated, staring at the lamp post with the beige light and I dreamed of becoming a star but not really knowing how or what to do to get to that point.

As a child, the only thing that matters is being able to play with your friends when you get to school and do the work in class when the teacher says to do it. I had dreams of being Randy Jackson's girlfriend when I got older. "The" Randy Jackson of the famous Jackson Five brothers. I made it a point to know everything about the brothers. My friend and I used to play this game when we were younger after school. We would pretend to be married to the brothers. She liked Marlon and of course, I liked Randy. The best thing about that game was we pretended to be sisters and our children were first cousins; then she added drama to the mix. The drama was I was supposedly having an affair with her husband, so she, in turn, had an affair with my husband, but she got pregnant. Those were the days. The game ended with both of us getting divorced from the ones we loved. Fun game...fun times. I wonder if she remembers us playing that game. In those days, every girl wanted to be married to the late Michael Jackson. He is dearly missed, but his music lives on. Growing up there weren't any real good role models to look up to. When I was 10, my mother brought home an Ebony magazine with a young lady on the cover by the name of Stacy Lattisaw. She was a new singer that just came onto the scene. Mother bought the magazine because (1) of her name, (2) to my mother, she was a very pretty girl, and (3) she was a rising star. My mother said to me, "I not only bought this because of her name but because I know that whatever you want in life, you can achieve whatever you set your mind to doing." I have been following her career since I was a preteen. She at a young age became my role model. Then, in December of that same year in 1979, I received the greatest gift ever given. Stacy Lattisaw's {Now Stacy Lattisaw Jackson}, cassette tape entitled *"With You"* Her voice was angelic. I listened to her every day and each time she came out with an album, I purchased it.

I sang in my former church choir for at least 32 years as a first soprano. There were times when I didn't want to sing. It had gotten so bad that it bothered me and I knew that if I stopped singing, I would lose that voice God had given me. Even though I wasn't blessed to actually become a singer, God used me in other ways that would bring me to where I am. I miss singing, but God knows what He is doing. Singing is a second love. When it scared me to the point of quitting, I pulled my best friend and cousin to the side and asked her to pray for me and she did. She understood that feeling. I am so thankful for having the opportunity to have had her in my life.

When I became of age to understand the meaning of love and wanting a boyfriend, I received that in due time. I would have to say that the young man who became my boyfriend had been my friend for six years prior to us getting together. As the saying goes, the first one is your first love-the second is your true love. Well, as fate would have it, the first relationship didn't last long due to the fact that he felt I talked too much. Not to everyone...just to him. As years passed, we remained friends and even tried to make it work once or twice, but it didn't. It took me three years to get over him. Mother took me shopping that day. She liked him because he was a gentleman. He understood my disability, helped me cope with it, pulled out chairs, opened doors and even cut my meat when it was necessary. He wasn't the only one who did that for me, though. The second one was a dream. He too was a gentleman. I was introduced to him by his father when I was 19. That relationship lasted almost two years. That was an on-and-off relationship as well. The breakup seemed long and this also took me three years to get over.

Relationship number three, I fell hard. He was a military man. He came to get me every other Friday to spend the weekend with him; I really enjoyed that time. He was *"my first."* We remained together for a year and five months; then, he returned to his home in New York. We remained in touch for two years after the breakup. He had the most gorgeous eyes. They were hypnotizing. I remember one Monday night when he brought me home; we were saying our goodbyes, and the moon was out; I smiled at him and he smiled back. For a moment, everything seems to go in slow motion.

He kissed me...He later told me that there was so much that he wanted to tell me, but he didn't want to ruin the moment. He was like a Prince Charming. I haven't had a night like that with anyone else since then. Of course, every man is different as you get older.

Each relationship I've had took three years to get over. That gives me time to collect my thoughts and get back to me. Just like every man, every relationship between a man and a woman takes time to get over. I had to learn how to adjust to being single. The last relationship, in my eyes, ended horribly because he didn't really love me. I was head over heels in love with this man ~ loved him too. I did everything to please him; I put myself aside just to make him happy, but I was doing it all wrong. I had put God on the back burner or what felt like it. I would pray thanking God for him being in my life. Even though I felt that this man was good for me...he wasn't and through that trial, I learned the hard way. Things started to change and I could see it. So, instead of asking God why? I asked Him to show me what I needed to do. And God did. For the next three months, this lesson had to be learned. God made me stronger when it was time and I asked the man I loved a question, and he gave an honest answer. A week later, I moved into my own apartment. Granted, we helped each other out when necessary, but it came down to it that I still had feelings even after dealing with another man who I hadn't met. The other man and I talked on the phone constantly and made plans to see each other. That never happened.

What tore me to pieces was a FaceBook status. I cried for hours. Sat outside, looked up at the dark sky and wondered why I even shed a tear over the man who didn't love me. I wasn't sad, hurt or angry. I didn't know what I was feeling, and then God whispered, "I know you spend time with me;

now I want you to spend more time with me." That's when I found out what my feelings were...my spirit was crushed. When that was revealed to me, I cried some more, wiped my tears, gave God thanks and went to bed. I continued my studies because of that just to have an understanding of myself, life and other people. Still, I had that desire to have someone special in my life to share my success with. Before all that, I must learn to love myself.

CHAPTER 6

Many Demands

<u>Job 42:4</u>: "Hear, I beseech thee, and I will speak: I will demand of thee, and declare thou unto me."

My pastor preached a sermon once and he mentioned that if you are wanting to get to know someone, you must ask questions. In my relationships that I've had down through the years, I've asked questions, but I suppose that they weren't the correct questions to ask when doing my best to get to know someone. It takes a very long time to get to know someone, and it doesn't matter how much time you spend with them; you are still learning about them each day you have the opportunity to spend with them. With my own falls of relationships, I learned to ask one question to wean out the bad apples. Everyone is different, so every question, every answer, and every prayer will not work the same for someone else. In order for you to get to the truth of the matter about someone, listen, observe and then come up with your own unique question or questions to ask a person so that you too can be able to wean out the bad apples. In this case, you must cut down all the trees before you enter deep into the woods. Don't go into the woods blindfolded and without an ax to chop down the trees.

There were demands placed on relationships as to what a person likes or dislikes. If that person didn't fit the bill, then there was no way that the person involved would last. I wear my heart on my sleeve and give anyone a chance. The demands: you can't have this, you can't have that, you can't do this, or you can't do that; you can't see this, you can't go there, let's do this and so forth. In one of my relationships, there came a point where everything that was done was questioned. I could barely talk to family members without being asked, "Who was that you were talking to? Your other man?" Then after a while, it became a game of explaining to that person that I wouldn't disrespect him by talking to someone else just because he had insecurity about the relationship. I never questioned him about the young ladies he introduced me to. I waited until he was ready to tell me who she was, and if he didn't tell, that would be on his conscience--not mine.

I now call my demands "requests" and give them to God. I was really being specific in my prayers, but each relationship that I thought was...wasn't. Then I looked back on those who came into my life. I've dated Virgos, Libras, Aries, Scorpios, and one Sagittarian like myself. Men, in general, love the chase and once they have you, they tend to get bored with you~ unless they really love you and desire to have a future with you. As one man boldly stated: "I just don't see us walking hand in hand down the aisle in holy matrimony...you are not what I am looking for." This was said after three years of being together. Yes, that broke my big heart to pieces, but I found enough strength to continue to love him during that time; now, I sometimes wonder what did I ever see in him? I laugh at myself with that thought because getting over the relationship was difficult at first. I found myself going gah-gah every time I saw him. So, to break that stronghold, I put a demand on myself. I demanded myself not to care anymore, I demanded myself not to answer the phone when he called, I demanded my heart to not swoon when I saw him, and I demanded myself to love me again. It took God's strength to help me through it and heal what was crushed.

Men have many demands. No, I am not a size eight, nor do I have long hair or perfect vision, but do you realize those things can fade away? This reminds me of what happened to me years ago. To make a long story short, after corresponding with this man, he sent a note stating how he knew he could get me to fall for him, how desperate some women are to get a man, that he was married and he would never go for the likes of me, and how ugly I was. So, I, in turn, blasted him and put everything that was written on the page, but it brought my esteem down quite a bit to the point where I don't really put my pictures up as a profile in many places. I learned my lesson, and I hope that he did as well. Still, I yearned for the relationship I desired. What's in the past will stay in the past.

I suppose women, too have demands as well as men when it comes to something they desire within a relationship. Instead of making demands, turn them into "requests."

CHAPTER 7

Darn Shame

<u>Ephesians 5: 12</u>: "For it is a shame even to speak of those things which are done of them in secret."

Has your parents ever told you, what is said in this house, stays in this house? Not that nothing was kept secret, especially from family, and it still applies today. Whatever you do inside the home should never be spread among the community or to one person; it would be just as well you told the whole community when you tell someone you think you trust. Okay, I was a blabbermouth and I got punished for it. Did I learn my lesson? Hmmm, that's a very good question. It took a minute to realize there are some things that are better left unsaid and undone. No, I'm not talking about leaving the kitchen a mess kind of "undone"; I am talking about doing things that you shouldn't do that you know better NOT to do. I was hell on wheels most of the time. It seemed to me that every day I got home, I was being whipped about something I did or said.

What I didn't understand was that just because I got punished for something that I didn't or did do, doesn't mean I go back to my friends telling them and laughing about it. That would get me into deeper trouble because, by the end of the day, mother seemed to know what was said and done by me. I had a cousin Velious Burns who I was just completely crazy about growing up as a child. He was a senior in high school, cursed like a sailor, and I loved listening to him talk. I took up this habit of cursing as well and I only did it on the bus. That only lasted for a few days until my mother got wind of me cursing and she once again punished me for using foul language, stating that she never wanted to hear of me doing that again. From that day on, I was somewhat of a reformed little girl.

I also told things that were personal that weren't supposed to be told. It has to be drilled in me or whipped out of me not to talk so much about family things. I am grateful for the whippings that I received as an adolescent. If it wasn't for those, I would be known as the woman to go to for gossip. That to me is destruction.

Sex is another story that needs to not only be done behind closed doors, but it's also a subject that should be kept to yourself between you and your loved one. The Bible says that we are to abstain from sex. {1 Corinthians 7:7} As a child growing up, I was afraid of it and I vowed to myself that I would never have sex until I got married. As years rolled by, my third relationship was a true test of faith for me and I failed. It has always been said, "be careful what you pray for...you just might get it." It came down to praying that I would stop being afraid of a man's manhood. At age 25, I had my first "real" sexual experience. Granted, he was extremely gentle with me but questioned me later about it. I tried my best to explain to him that I wanted to stop being afraid of "it" and that he was truly the first for me. We remained together for a year and five months. I wanted to have his children. School came first, and I was just starting over in college. I loved this man and I wanted to spend every waking moment with him.

During my stint in college, I ran across one of my exes who was also taking college courses. I noticed him on campus and spoke and for him it seemed like his whole world stood still. I say this because once I said hello, whoever he was talking to, he stopped mid-sentence and it was as if he finally saw someone who he had wanted to see for years. He quickly said his goodbyes to the other person and held the door open for me. Over the course of a few months, I began to trust him. He made the suggestion that since we were headed in the same direction, I might as well ride with him to keep from having my mother pick me up. This idea sounded good to me since we were friends. Then after a while, things started to change with his thoughts. He felt that he was getting too close and he had to back away from me. Four days later, he said that we needed to talk. Not really knowing the seriousness of what was on his mind, the ride home was quiet. He spoke with me outside and then we said our goodbyes.

The next few minutes felt like a movie going in slow motion. He walked into the house, stating that he just couldn't stay away. He grabbed me from behind and pushed me toward the kitchen sink. I begged him to stop, but he proceeded to undo my pants and his while pressing my body against the sink. Imagine a 5'10, 250lbs of weight pressed against you. When I told him that I would tell, he laughed, saying, "Tell...who you gonna tell? If you do tell, no one will believe you. I will just say that I was with my boys. You can scream all you want; no one can hear you. And if I find out you told, I will come back and kill you. At this point, he had his hands around my throat, continuing to force his way inside me--hurting me. When he was done, he stood back laughing, zipping up his pants and saying, "You know you wanted this big piece of meat inside of you." And with that, he walked out of the door.

August 26, 1991, I shut down...

CHAPTER 8

The "Duh" Transformation Of Abundance

John 10:10: **"The thief cometh not, but for to steal, and to kill, and to destroy: I am come that they might have life, and that they might have it more abundantly."**

Thinking about my mentor's videos, Ms. Abiola Abrams, and one in particular {Fake It Til You Make It} I've been spending my time listening to abundance recordings and writing, and it occurred to me that my life is abundant. Just like Oprah's "Aha Moment," I am calling mine "The Duh Transformation." What I mean by that is the fact that while listening to a video of what was being said, I realized that I have an abundance already in my life. What I AM doing my best to understand is how to apply it to "Fake It Til You Make It" advice. The saying is you *have* because the Father in Heaven has and "The Lord is my Shepherd I shall not want." Which an expert raised a good question: Can you let go of wanting just so you can have? My sister and mother were talking about things we pray for to be manifested and not having a pity party. The conversation began with seeing a report on the news about darker-skinned children feeling dumb because they are not light-skinned. My sister went on to say that her seven-year-old son was asked the question by his dad {they have been married for 21 years now} who is the smartest, darker-skinned or lighter-skinned? Keep in mind that he didn't watch the news report. My nephew's response was, "we are all the same." So the question was repeated and his answer remained the same, and then he went on to say that "just because you are darker doesn't make you dumb or smarter." He and another boy are the top two smartest in his class and the other boy is White. They don't have a difference between each other because of color. They are the only two who participate in class. My niece and nephew inspire me to be determined in what I do. And they, in turn, tell me on a daily basis I inspire them and how beautiful I am.

Many experts say to concentrate on what you have and not what you don't have. My thought has always been since I was able to understand it, for what reason is it I don't have a man in my life? Then I look at many relationships I observe that are unhealthy...then I think, God still may be preparing that man for me; he IS around somewhere. I've had these dreams of being at celebrity parties and the people know who I AM. The most recent dream was me being engaged to Randy Jackson {the late Michael Jackson's brother}. I've been crazy about him since I was 15. :-) In this dream, there was an elaborate gathering that he put together. Oprah and Gail were there; Lil Kim, Nicki Minaj, Mr. Powell {from Next Friday}, Mr. Lindo, my family...but for some reason, I was with Ms. Winfrey. Randy's ex was there and I was told to give her the roses that I had ~ split them between her and I. And the other roses were to go to Randy. As the dream continued, a huge gunfight broke out over the roses...in the end, Randy's ex and I found Randy and became friends. Come to find out; the roses had something to do with my engagement ring, which Randy's ex had for safekeeping. {Marlon and Tito were there} The fight broke out between Powell, Lindo, Lil Kim and Nicki ~ they too had something to do with the roses and the ring.

And the ETF recording that Ms. Abiola Abrams did...I found something else for meditating that the Jewish community does. With Dr. Baskaran Pillai. It is amazing!!!!!

I came to terms with this guy who contacted me after 19 years stating that he wanted to start over with me; he's still doing the same things he did 19 years ago and calls himself an evangelist; that's when I got off the phone with him one night and a calmness came over me about the situation...and I told myself that I wasn't going to put myself through that again with him. I went from abundance to nephew, to dream, to a man. My point being...I also realize that abundance doesn't have to mean money or having a man in my life.

It occurred to me that my abundance comes from having a family, friends, my own place, food in my refrigerator, clothes on my back, money in the bank {what there is of it}, the ability to walk, talk, see, touch, taste, feel, read and write. This is a thought process that you have to keep in mind when you are feeling down. This is your wealth and your prosperity; everyone's prosperity is different, be it with or without much money. When you think about these things, you can become more grateful and happy with your life.

CHAPTER 9

Level Up

Psalms 19:14: **"Let the words of my mouth, and the meditation of my heart, be acceptable in thy sight, O Lord, my strength, and my redeemer."**

Dedicated to DeKelton L. Lester

I take things to heart; when that happens, I get stressed out. There is this saying in the Christian community, "Too blessed to be stressed," but we all know that when trials come, we become torn up inside. The Bible comes into play when we need God to speak to us. Sit and be still. Let Him talk to you. I even found myself taking on other meditation habits. I really do need to be careful because I have extremely bad nerves. I have heard that some meditation practices can and cannot be good for you. It feels like I've tried them all...then again, maybe not. Check with your physician first before going into anything such as meditation.

In order to meditate, there must be an abundance of quiet around you, a clear mind to focus specifically on the person's words whom you are listening to if there is an audio you do by. Breathing is also meditating. The same rules apply when it comes to that technique. Your health is the most important. Yoga is definitely good for anyone's body. I was diagnosed with this condition called Fibromyalgia years ago. I was given test after test after test. It is stated to be a clinical condition that affects the nerves. The pain is real. Exercising was hard on me. Then I ran across a therapy that was perfect for my pain. Viniyoga from the expert guidance of Gary Kraftsow. Dr. Gary Kraftsow is one of the world's leading Yoga therapists and designer of the only Yoga practices that are effective for back pain in a National Institutes of Health-sponsored clinical study. This technique was found to be the best therapy for Fibromyalgia.

It seems to be a different form of yoga for areas of the body that are in pain. I started off slow, doing at least 10 minutes until I was able to work up to 30-minute increments that were on the video. The poses are done all the way through on the floor and not held long. These positions gave me so much satisfaction and made me feel great afterward. Breathing techniques were involved in this as well. I took the medicine that was prescribed for me, but it kept me sleeping. I have to take it, though. In the mornings or afternoons that I rise, I give thanks to God for being my watchman and allowing me to see another day to do what I do. He wants us not to worry about things and to remember that He is in control.

You have the right to reach a higher level in whatever type of meditation you choose to help you make it through your day. Just continue to breathe and give thanks.

CHAPTER 10

Pick A Number ~ Any Number

Numbers 15:12: "According to the number that ye shall prepare, so shall ye do to EVERYONE according to their number.**

What does the lottery, apartments, social security, ages, and driver's licenses have in common? They all contain numbers. If you stop to think about it, you and your life are nothing but a number. Numbers make you follow rules. Numbers make you pay a bill. Numbers make you stand in line. Numbers will have you do all sorts of things. Numbers can even lead your life. In two recent numerology studies it has shown me what my life was made up of. How numerology is done: numerologists take your name and date of birth using numbers, then break the numbers down and add them together to come up with your life path number, expression and urge.

According to one reading sent to me, it read as such; my life path is number 9: "You have a charismatic and very open personality that attracts you a lot of friends. You are very social, sometimes at the expense of your other responsibilities...You are a deeply spiritual individual who often displays a deep interest in religion or the occult at a very early age. In fact, many nines grow up to be psychics, healers, priests and nuns. You probably feel responsible for keeping up the morality or spirit of mankind in some way or even responsible for their very souls. This is why many nines also end up working for the law as policemen or judges or in some aspect of spiritual or psychological counseling.

The emphasis of your life path is on finding ways to communicate the divinity of man in a practical context. As many nines are also very artistic, this connection with the higher powers might also be expressed through talents such as writing, music or painting.

At some point in your life, you have probably sworn to yourself to make this world a better place. You are extremely compassionate and feel above the matters that you feel causes factions of society to be divided. You are very aware of feeling as insignificant as a grain of sand in the Universe and believe that materialism, prejudice and lust just don't matter in the long run. You have a charismatic and very open personality that attracts you a lot of friends. You are very social, sometimes at the expense of your other responsibilities. Sometimes a number nine might take too much time out during the day "to smell the flowers" and incur the resentment of those that are left to pick up the slack.

Your attitude towards life, in general, is very selfless and you usually have a good connection with God or a higher power. However, often the number 9 faces a unique challenge at some point in his or her life that seems to be a test of faith. Usually, this incident takes the form of a devastating personal loss, disease or some sort of tragedy. This triggers a period of time that lasts a few years that is often called the "dark night of the soul." It is usually during this period of your life that you find the extreme courage and strength to become what is called a wounded healer.

Your life may seem too tough to handle at times which makes you vulnerable to finding substitutes for the family unit. As you are naturally very lonely and insecure, you are particularly vulnerable to joining a cult or becoming fanatical in the religious sense.

If you are a number nine, you may find your life seems more difficult than others. This is because it is common human nature to take advantage of your compassion, empathy and generosity. It may seem unfair to you that others do not appreciate the spiritual gifts that you have to offer, especially when you demand so little materially from the world. This is part of the problematic path of the number 9, who is often fated to learn that the path of true compassion does not necessarily result in spiritual rewards for the healer either.

Although you may feel quite clear about your divine purpose and goals in life, others may perceive you as weird or spacey. This is why it is often difficult for a number 9 to keep a job for long. Relationships might also be very difficult for a 9 to sustain, as this particular path is a rather lonely one. Part of the 9's spiritual development is usually being presented with situations that force them to let go of emotional situations and connections that might interfere with the higher purpose that the cosmos has in store for them."

My expression is calculated a little differently. This describes the potential natural talents and abilities. My expression number is 5 and reads as such: "You are also very accepting of new people and new ideas. The last thing that could ever be said of you is that you are closed-minded... You are optimistic, inquisitive, and embrace change. You are a freedom-loving individual who expresses their love of independence, often through a bohemian or unusual lifestyle. You are blessed with a brilliant creative mind that is never at a loss for a solution to a problem.

As your independence is so important to you, you thrive best in creative occupations that allow you a great deal of travel. You have an eye for design and appreciate the good things in life. In fact, you may spend a lot of your time trying to figure out how to get these things without having to work too hard.

If you are a typical five, then you will meet with the most success by selling some aspect of yourself or your talent. The height of your personal expression is in your talent for persuasion. This is why you are best suited for jobs in media, marketing and design.

You very much believe that a person is defined by what he does and not what he wants to do, so any business or project that you start will be very much branded with your personal flair. It is a number 5 that tends to name a business after himself or send out a resume with a photo.

When it comes to business, you also tend to have a "hands-on" approach as you rely a lot on your wit, charm and good looks to get what you want. Once the deal is sealed, however, you sometimes have difficulty seeing it through to completion. This is because your brilliant mind is captured by so many other interests that it is difficult for you to focus sometimes.

Sometimes your need to express your independence brings you to a critical point in both your professional and personal relationships. You are terrified of being stuck in one place or having your free spirit suffocated by labels and possessiveness. For this reason, many of you feel quite suffocated in relationships or are unable to hold down a day job for any length of time.

You are very popular socially because you are the life of every party. You have a light nimble mind and excellent verbal skills. You also have enormous powers of analysis that give you an edge when it comes to investing money, judging others and avoiding harmful situations.

You are also very accepting of new people and new ideas. The last thing that could ever be said of you is that you are closed-minded. You will try anything once and you often respond willingly to a dare. However, sometimes your permissiveness leads to relationships with odd or unstable individuals.

Romantically, others may find you hard to get close to as you would rather sit and chat than get intimate. Others fail to understand that the most valued expression of your love is the expression of your hopes and dreams to another.

You are also very pragmatic when it comes to all of your relationships and believe in treating everyone equally. Deep down, you are very philosophical about relationships and believe that no person should be so important that he or she should have the power to make you happy or sad. This can often distress your soul mate, who doesn't feel that special in your presence. Part of your challenge might be showing through your actions how loving all without sacrificing one can be achieved."

The Soul Urge is your "Heart's Desire," what you desire to be, to have and to do in your life. That number turned out to be an 11. My soul urge reads like this: "Your soul's purpose is to manifest ideals into reality, but usually, such an endeavor means that you must be a catalyst for change. For this reason, many who encounter you actually fear you as what you suggest and say is a threat to their emotional and physical security. However, this does not usually bother you as you have an innate realization that without chaos, there can be no personal transformations or betterment of society.

Your highest calling is to become the master of a religion or of a spiritual realm. This can be a painful process emotionally as it often means stripping away of the personality and ego. Many elevens travel a very difficult path, fraught with personal, physical and financial obstacles as the cosmos tests their mettle to have faith only in their higher self.

You are the ultimate seeker of truth and will go to any lengths to find a spiritual teacher or guru. This search often leads you on a path that is full of many pitfalls and disappointments as you realize that one spiritual system doesn't work for you or that a guru or teacher is only human after all. However, by the end of your life, you are fated to acquire a great deal of practical and esoteric wisdom. Many of you become as hard and clear as diamonds when it comes to your clarity about the human race.

You also have the highest ideals of any other number and therefore set yourself up for disappointment. Many of you are born to be very sensitive emotionally and many of your soul lessons have to do with detaching emotionally from the pain and misery of the human race. Common soul lessons learned by number 11s are not to take things personally, to realize that everything, including happiness, is transitional and to realize that nothing is perfect (especially humans.) At the beginning of their lives, elevens are often very attached to people, but by the end, they usually achieve an omniscient emotional distance that is more beneficial and healing for a large group of humans than just a few.

Often your search for spiritual truth leads you to experiment with mind-altering drugs. You are fascinated with the idea of altering your consciousness to achieve enlightenment. Rather than drugs, teachings from a master or trips to holy or mystical places would better cultivate your talents.

One of the dangers of being an eleven is that you think your psyche can take in anything and not suffer damage. Some of the spiritual experiences that you desire may be too strong for your delicate nervous system. For this reason, you need to avoid mind-altering drugs, situations that are too extreme or religions that invite you to host dead spirits. You are also more vulnerable to astral attacks than the other numbers simply because you are like a wide-open channel that is willing to receive psychic information from others. As some psychic information is destructive, you need to learn meditation and psychic protection techniques to shield yourself from negative influences and energies.

As you are so curious, it is very easy for you to be led down the wrong spiritual path. If this does happen, you are better off to forgive yourself and move on rather than dwelling on a mistake that you think may have ruined your life. Testing your faith with negative spiritual influences is another way that the cosmos assures that you will eventually learn to transcend the ego desires of your personality."

CHAPTER 11

Pick A Number ~ Any Number (Part II)

<u>Numbers 15:12</u>: "According to the number that ye shall prepare, so shall ye do to everyone according to their number."

The second reading was given by Mr. Aiden Powers. A master numerologist from Manhattan, New York. I loved his readings the best. My life path and expression numbers were the same, but I found that my soul urge number was a bit disappointing; nonetheless, I am grateful for how it all came out. His results read as such: "You are a natural leader, and you assume that you are in charge even if you are not. If you are out in public, people may mistake you for someone who works for the establishment you are visiting by your confidence and know-how. You will take care of everyone else, but you need to learn to speak up when you need help. You often feel unloved or abandoned by your mother or father, or you may feel completely responsible for them. It's maybe hard for you to let go of the past because of this.

You are focused on humanitarian efforts. You have an extremely strong sense of sympathy and kindness. You are unselfish and helping others is very important to you. You do not just want to help those in need but feel a very strong sense of what they are going through, which provides a greater incentive for your cause.

You are a friendly person and people like you because of this. Your charity knows no bounds, and you give freely of your money, time, and energy. You strive and dream of working for a better world. Because you are so giving, you may realize that your money life may struggle.

You may also have a tendency to be scattered-brained, which is why your talents lie in so many different directions. This is why you may find it difficult to focus on just one job or skill that you can sharpen. If you are not following your Life Path and are instead pursuing materialistic gains, you could feel a deep level of dissatisfaction with yourself.

The number 9 symbolizes endings and spiritual perception. You can overcome a lot, and you are often required to do so in your lifetime. You are an individual who finds comfort in completion and resolution. You will need to make choices and not resist endings."

The Expression reads this way: "You are a non-conformist. You love to revolutionize your surroundings with adventure and enthusiasm. You love your independence. Freedom is centered around which your life revolves. You need it for your endurance.

By using freedom properly, you are able to discover and expand all of your varied skills. You will meet a slew of people and travel far distances from where you started. Freedom is the ambiance essential for you to bring forth your many talents. Only by avoiding the incarceration of deceptive security are you able to bring forth your abilities.

You are unusually flexible. In fact, change is your saving grace, as in the same way, you need challenge and variety. You hate the habit of life and being stuck is a disaster for you. You become unhappy when you are held back or held down. The taste and texture and color of life have an overwhelming appeal for you.

You are the type who will try everything at least twice in life. Thus, all of life is a party for your senses, but this can get you into trouble. You may fail to respect your usual limits, either physically or within society. Any sort of boundary is an abhorrence to you, which can blind you to your practical limits and may cause you to act in excess toward your desire for food, sweets, alcohol, sex, and drugs.

My Soul Urge from his reading turned out to be a 4, and it reads: "You like to live your life with consistency, leaning more on the need for stable relationships and projects. You hate when change comes suddenly because you prefer orderliness in all things. You are rigorous with the details and quite careful to look before you leap. You want to be reliable, a picture of power and an example of an order for others.

You require and wish for as much love as you can get, but you are not very affectionate. You can be a little cold to those you want love from. You detest liars as truth is held in high regard for you and you find people trying to impress you to be silly.

You can be very strong-minded and firm with your decisions. Try not to lose sight of the larger picture and dream while you examine the depths of the bottom line.

Work is very important to you and your life, but you may have the problem of overworking and forgetting of other emotional needs. You may not realize how easy it is for you to become a workaholic if you're not careful. Yet, you have a great deal of vigor and can accomplish a lot once you set your mind to it.

Being flexible is your key to accord and balance in life for yourself and others. Yet you must realize that others do not share your same nature for the well-oiled machine. In fact, they may feel largely repulsed and uncomfortable with it. Just remember that the peace you get from tidiness may represent a prison to someone else.

You are gifted in your ability to converse. Your ability with words is almost limitless. You can be a salesman, politician, lawyer, public relations person, and minister. You also possess the talent to share and go forward with new ideas. You love the fresh and inexperienced. Your field is the open frontier. You are a bit of a gambler and often play for very high stakes. You like to work with others but need to perform your task with an imaginative mindset by the restraints of others.

You are intelligent and a quick thinker, but your thought processes is mostly unorganized and scattered. You must stay focused if you want to be flourishing. You fall in and out of love frequently, especially early in life. These distinctive character traits usually make for a lively and thrilling love life, but you must guard against trivial feelings and associations. Your challenge is to create and maintain lasting relationships that are not superficial.

Willpower and setting healthy limits is the key to your success in virtually every area of your life. Ironically, you will find that as you learn to set suitable limits on yourself, you will develop more self-actualizing traits and realize even greater freedom.

Your tendency is to give up once you've got a project or job under control because you grow bored quickly. You start to fantasize about a new challenge or the rewards of your great accomplishment long before the work is finished. It is no secret that you desire the whole world.

You are aware that you have many talents that can bring much success. But that success depends on your willingness to choose certain areas to concentrate on and to bring them to perfection.

Do keep in mind that these readings are for entertainment purposes only, but within the numbers, you do see yourself, your life and what you have

done.

- 37 -

CHAPTER 12

Consequences

<u>Revelations 2:5</u>: "Remember therefore from whence thou art fallen, and repent, and do the first works; or else I will come unto thee quickly, and will remove thy candlestick out of his place, except thou repent."

When a person does something that he or she knows is wrong, later on down the road, there will be things that will cause him or her to suffer. Keep in mind that no one is perfect and no other should judge that person. Jesus wants us to be perfect, so there will be times when God does show a person favor and gives grace and mercy. For example, someone steals something that doesn't belong to him or her. The ending result is the person would be sent to jail. Or if someone doesn't pay a speeding or parking ticket. Taking office supplies is a federal offense, BUT it's still stealing.

I have never been to jail for any reason, but there were still results of me not doing what I was supposed to do in my life. Even though I did graduate high school with a "B" average, there was one class in that I was put back. The teachers were in the office laughing about the fact that my mother came to the school and spoke to the principal. This particular teacher even spoke about it in class with the other students, which was wrong. I went straight home and told my mother what this teacher had said and she was right back in the principal's office again to speak with him about the teacher's behavior.

College was a bit different. It seemed much harder. The first year was fantastic. I always did good in my first semester. After my first year and a half in college, I decided to transfer because the major I was taking was only for that time period. I wanted to go to my aunt's alma mater in Commerce, Texas. My dream of following in her footsteps and desiring to be like her was a dream come true. I know, I know...I should be more like Jesus. I see it as He gave me someone to look up to. Still, to this day, part of me desires to be like her.

I majored in Communications, not knowing where it would lead me. I had so many dreams and accomplished some goals. My dream was to one day sit beside Mr. Tom Brokaw, learn from him and be the best that I could be. Meeting him would be a dream come true. On my first test in Radio & Television, I made a 90. I was so proud of that 90. All tests after that I struggled with, and eventually, I had to go home. My instructors, however, saw the determination and drive I had for the course. All the grant money wasn't gone and I could have retaken the course as offered, but I didn't get that opportunity, so back home I went.

I immediately applied for college courses here and took on more than I could chew. Loving English Composition, every grade that I seemed to get was a failing grade but determined to bring that grade up. Eventually, I had to drop out because of my failing grades. Yes, I was a college dropout, but it was a wonderful experience. Knowing that there was something for my life, I attended college again after a year or so of waiting. I went back to college, majoring in Office Careers. In that course were many subjects that would boggle the mind. Granted, I had to retake Accounting and passed it the second time. I graduated in 1994. Still not satisfied with doing things that I did, I took an at-home study course, "Break Into Writing." My instructor's name was Ms. Ann Rice. No, not THE Anne Rice, who wrote:

"Interview With A Vampire," but Ms. Rice has been an asset to the Long Ridge Writing Group community for as long as I've gotten to know her as an instructor. I graduated in May 2000. I put my writing to good use, looking for publishing companies that will publish my work. I searched high and low until I came across a company that gave me an opportunity to be heard. In 2004, "Cold Hearted Warm Hearted" was published. I enjoyed the sales and recognition of the success of the book. I was yet, not done. I desired to do more, feel more, and reach more. Then the next flood of words came. I wrote when the feeling hit. It seemed like time had passed. I was miserable because nothing seemed to happen for me. With fervent prayer and writing out ideas and plans, I decided to take action. I knew that I couldn't do what needed to be done where I was, so I moved and prepared myself for what was going to happen.

In September 2010, I moved out of my grandmother's home. Three months later, I moved into my own place. During that time, I came across an associate who gave me his editor's number and told me that my work needed to be out and how good it was. I gave her a call, explained my situation, and began the birth of "Rejuvenation: Innocent Until Proven Guilty." My second "baby" was born on February 14, 2012.

During the time that I had moved out of my grandmother's home, my mother and I did not speak for a while. I couldn't make her see this was something that had to be done, and it was time. I was in constant prayer about that situation. When there was trouble on the forefront with my "so-called" relationship, I stayed on my knees until I got an answer. Each Sunday, I was given a message that helped me out tremendously. This particular Sunday, taking my problems to the altar, eyes filled with tears, I didn't see my mother there. She came up to me, wrapped her arms around me, and I just melted into her arms. I knew then God had answered my prayers. All because I stood back and let Him work. I thought I lost her...I didn't.

CHAPTER 13

Beauty Inside Out

<u>Numbers 6:26</u>: "The Lord lift up his countenance upon THEE AND give thee peace."

Did you ever stop to think how God has blessed us all, no matter what we go through? We get so wrapped up in "us," family, friends and work that sometimes we forget to give God praise for what we do have. He wants us to slow down and take in all the beauty that surrounds us each and every day. Easier said than done, right? The time that you get up in the morning to make yourself that first cup of coffee or get on that treadmill to work out is the time that you should stop, take a deep breath, and silently give thanks because God has shown you favor.

Sometimes, I get so caught up in my financial situation that God is pushed back further and further, but the wonderful thing about God is that He is all strong and mighty. He pushes His way back to the forefront of your brain, reminding you that He is still in control...Well, to me, He does. When you have troubles, He still gives us all grace and new mercies. The Bible verses on the subject of worrying. We should not worry about what we should eat, drink or wear, for tomorrow will take care of itself. God doesn't want us to worry. The Bible also says God's yoke is easy and His burden is light. He is telling you that you can go to Him at any time when something is going on in your life. But keep in mind that He also wants you to go to Him in your good times. Your good times should outweigh your bad.

We should also bear one another's burdens. This doesn't mean that you run to your friends with your problems all the time. You both may have the same thing going on. This means you should share your experience with your friend once God has brought you through that situation. You are responsible for your own actions. It is on you when you fall short of doing what you are supposed to do.

In my grandmother's dictionary of her Bible, countenance meant beauty. But in the NLT version of the written word, it means favor. God shows us His favor every day. Or you could think about it in this way the beauty of His favor will give us peace. When I finally learned that for myself, I learned to love myself better as a person, a human being and a woman.

CHAPTER 14

Double Double Toil And Trouble

<u>John 8:32</u>: And ye shall know the truth, and the truth shall make you free.

Growing up, my sister, aunt, and I were taught to tell the truth because truth helped being saved from much heartache and building lies on top of lies. When a child knows he or she is going to get into trouble, a few won't tell the truth because they are afraid that the punishment will be extremely harsh. Oftentimes, it's not. We had to be punished to be taught a lesson. That lesson was: Not telling the truth will only get you in deeper trouble. Nowadays, children will heighten the lie just to see what they can get away with.

The truth always has two sides. It can either help you, harm you or both. Let us go with a good scenario; like if someone was booked on charges, the police would give the person in custody an option to tell the truth to reduce the sentence or if not, he would serve time. If the person squeals, their life would be in danger from what was told. With parents, the truth is always warranted. There is no way to get out of trouble with parents, so children might as well tell the truth.

Okay, so I am no angel. I have told things to my parents just to get myself out of trouble, only to get into more trouble for lying. Later on, in years, I found that being too honest can lead to trouble as well. This actually takes me back to the story in the Bible, where Peter denied Jesus three times. It was already told by Jesus that before the cock crows, Peter will deny Him three times. With that story in mind as a child growing up, I awoke to the sounds of a rooster crowing. This sound always frightened me because in my mind at that age, it meant something bad was going to happen. I always prayed that the sound of the rooster crowing wouldn't really mean anything bad and that God would take the fear away. Just knowing that someone-- even a disciple denying Jesus would cause so much pain makes you wonder why people lie in the first place. It has always been said that *things happen for a reason.* Peter was afraid to die and Jesus had to die to save us. Picture this: Peter following in the distance when Jesus was arrested, sat down by a fire when he was noticed first by a woman who blurted out, "This man was with Jesus." Peter said, "Woman, I don't know him." Then someone else said, "You are one of them." Peter said again, "Man, I am not!"

The Bible goes on to say that an hour later, someone else recognized Peter and Peter replied, "Man, I don't know what you're talking about." This is from the NIV translation. We say the same exact words at times when we either try to understand something or get out of something. Just as Peter said his last word or as he was speaking, the rooster crowed. The Lord turned and looked straight at Peter; he remembered what the Lord told him and Peter went out, as the Bible says, "and wept bitterly." Can you see Peter crying like a big baby because he knew he had done something wrong and couldn't take it back? Now, imagine lying to get out of trouble. Where does that lead you? And where does that lead the other person?

Lying about something can put an innocent person in jail. It can also get someone injured or killed. Honesty can also get someone injured or killed. There really is no way to avoid not telling the truth to stay out of trouble, but there is good news. The good news is when God is on your side, and you are on His side, you can withstand any kind of trouble that comes your way and it will come your way as long as you are living.

Did I ever lie? Of course, I did. About what? Anything that I thought would get and keep me out of trouble. In fact, lying just made things worse for me. So, I decided to change that to become as honest as I could possibly be. I then found out that being honest still got me into trouble. Don't you love it when a parent tells you, "If you just tell the truth, I promise I won't punish you?" They say that until they hear the extent of your truth. So, does that mean they "lied" to you? They are the parents... Remember that.

CHAPTER 15

BE CAREFUL WHO YOU SLEEP WITH

Genesis 30:19: And Leah conceived again and bare Jacob the sixth son.

Jacob had a thing for Leah's sister, Rachel. Jacob was only looking at the exterior of Rachel. He served seven years to make her his wife. To Jacob's surprise, he was given the oldest daughter instead who was Leah. The Bible describes her as "tender-eyed," meaning she had weak eyes. Seeing that he was tricked by the sister's father, he agreed to serve another seven years to his wife, Rachel. God saw that Leah was hated, so God opened her wound while Rachel was barren. Leah was favored by God to have children. She, her handmaid, Rachel's handmaid, and Rachel gave Jacob a total of 12 children. Anyone who knows of this story will find that this chapter will not be about jealousy, relatives, or the beauty of the person. The two chapters in the Bible spoke of beauty and jealousy between the sisters.

This story is a sad one because the fairest of the two sisters was hated while the other one was loved. In that country, then, the rules were that a man marries the oldest daughter first. In God's eyes, Leah was beautiful and could have been smart, but things happen for a reason. Women and men today can't seem to get along because of the children who are being born. The women are either saying that the fathers are deadbeat dads and refuse to let the fathers see their children, or the men are calling the women crazy. If there is no marriage, then there is no unity between the two individuals who conceived the child, and the child suffers.

At what point do you decide that you want to have children? Think before you lie down, especially if it's with someone that is random. You know the ones? The ones who are just there in the heat of the moment. Yes, children are gifts from God no matter how they are conceived~ the wrong or the right way. A man needs to hold up his part of the parenting by doing all he can to help the woman. The woman should not throw anything in the man's face about the child and refuse him the right to see the child. The child will then grow up despising one of the parents just because of hearsay.

It's not fair to blame one parent because things didn't work out. Then the man or the woman is seen as evil and constantly talked about. The child grows up with the idea that the parent doesn't really love him or her. That thought has been placed into the child's mind that she or he is not loved, and then it is shown that he or she isn't loved by the actions of the other parent. It tears the child any many different directions.

There was a time when I was told that I wasn't college material and that my dad was to blame. As a young woman, those words were harsh, but as I got older, I realized that those were only words and they could be forgotten because I knew I wasn't dumb; everyone has a problem with a class they just don't understand. I wondered the reason for the statement ... I held on to that for the longest time because I literally felt like I didn't need to be in college, but I loved learning. I kept going until I got it right. Even today, I have this desire to return to college AGAIN for the sixth time and major in business. If I don't, I will continue to wonder what it's like to take a class in Business.

I wanted to prove a point that I was smart enough to finish and have something to show for it. Yes, after all the hard work, I received my Associate Degree. I want a higher degree because most jobs want the person to have a certain degree and experience to get hired. On down the line, the most important thing is whose you are or belong to, not about a title.

What's important to you? Being God's child? A title? Who your parents are, or what has been said?

CHAPTER 16

Praise Him Through The Pain

Matthew 9: 2 And, behold, they brought to him a man sick of the palsy, lying on a bed: and Jesus seeing their faith said unto the sick of the palsy; Son, be of good cheer; thy sins be forgiven thee.

I chose this scripture because, just like this man in the Bible, I have Palsy. I have Cerebral Palsy. This is a birth defect that damages the brain. I didn't know what it was until I was 10 years old or the name of it. So, I took my trusted encyclopedia and looked it up. In the 1970's it was described as a birth defect that happens during birth. Today it is stated by many that the "lack of oxygen to the brain or trauma to the head during labor and delivery can cause Cerebral Palsy. If the infant does not get enough oxygen, the brain can be injured." I went through life as a normal child at home. I did chores, played games, even got into trouble, and was disciplined for my wrongdoings. It was the outside world that was so mean and unforgiving. My doctor and family called me a miracle child because I wasn't supposed to live. Cerebral Palsy can also cause death as well. But God let me stay here for a reason. Would you believe I'm still trying to figure out that reason? We all have a purpose in life and it is up to us to figure out what that purpose is.

I also realize that with having Cerebral Palsy comes other illnesses, but late in life is when it all happened. I started having fainting spells and didn't know what was causing them. Stress? No. Too much exercise? No. Cerebral Palsy? It is a possibility, but the doctors aren't even sure. Then I was told that I had asthma and that asthma could be the reason for the fainting spells which now goes back to stress. I first went to a doctor who stated that a "dumping syndrome" was causing the fainting spells or it was the after-effects from passing out. The pain would start in the lower abdominal area and not move. This, in turn, would cause dizziness, stopped-up ears and ringing in the ears. **Phase One:** No, I did not just pass out! **Phase two:** coming to and realizing that I did pass out. **Phase three:** pass out again. **Phase four:** using the bathroom. These episodes went on for quite some time over a period of six to seven years. The "dumping syndrome" stopped, but that wasn't what was going on with my body.

I was given a nerve test, but at that time, everything seemed to be fine. The fainting spells continued while I was living at home. It skipped a year or two and started again. I continued to see my doctors, who were specialists in this field. Both doctors kept an eye on me just in case there were any drastic changes. January 2011 became more of a drastic year for me. I moved into my own place and acquired more hurt. Don't get me wrong ~ during this whole time of all the pain and near-death experiences, I prayed to God and gave Him thanks for seeing me through everything that made me sick. One night in January, I ended up on the floor in the fetal position, riddled with pain. My hands were literally closed because of cramping. I cried...both of my feet were in the same type of pain and I couldn't move. I laid on the floor...praying while in pain. By God's grace, I was able to make it to the bathroom to warm up my hands enough to be able to dial the phone for the ambulance.

I am a big woman and EMT had to carry me to the ambulance. After so much testing, the results came back fine. The doctor said, "whatever you did, it helped the situation." I was given pain medicine and sent home. This pain continued until the winter of the year and I was diagnosed with Fibromyalgia. Before then, I was given medicines for pains that I didn't understand and why I would hurt all over. Some mornings I wasn't able to move. The first doctor couldn't explain why I was having so much pain and he narrowed it down to it being caused by my Cerebral Palsy. I didn't want to accept that as an answer, but he was my doctor. I, in turn, searched for a second opinion, and it was given to me after extensive testing.

I had to change my way of thinking, eating, and living. It doesn't happen overnight. This is a lifestyle now. The pain from Fibromyalgia, before knowing I had it, had been going on for five years. I noticed that there was swelling in my shoulder area and it wouldn't go down for days or even weeks. Then, the pain came. I was told it was a muscle spasm in between the L4 and L5 vertebrae that caused the pain, which made it look like arthritis, but it wasn't arthritis because my body felt like pins and needles set on fire going into my skin. I don't wish that kind of pain on anyone.

I have also read that Cerebral Palsy can eventually cause Fibromyalgia. Granted, I am NOT a doctor, but it's hard to diagnose something else when something else is going on inside your body. I found out that as far as Cerebral Palsy is concerned, I am not alone in having it. I am one out of 1 million people who has this birth defect. Dan Keplinger, a critically acclaimed artist from Maryland who is not only my friend of many years but was told he would never be a good painter by his instructors, but he beat the odds. I am very proud of him. Abbey Nicole Curran represented Iowa at Miss USA 2008 and now holds a position as chairman of her own non-profit pageant, "The Miss You Can Do It Pageant," for young girls and women with special needs; Anne McDonald, an Australian author; Bonner Paddock became the first to reach the summit of the tallest mountain in the world; Chris Fonseca a comedian who has written for the likes of Jerry Seinfeld, Rosanne Arnold and Jay Leno; Christy Brown an Irish author, painter and poet who had his story told in the movie "My Left Foot;" Geri Jewell, a comedian and actress was one of the first whom I knew to have Cerebral Palsy. Seeing her in her stand-up comedy act on television, I remember her wearing a shirt that read, "I'm Not Drunk, I Have Cerebral Palsy." She became my strength in knowing that I could accomplish anything in life. There is a list of well-known people with this disability and I hope to join that list to also make a difference a people's lives. It doesn't stop our lives; it makes us better and stronger.

CHAPTER 17

Not There Yet

<u>John 5:40</u>: Yet you refuse to come to me to receive this life.

Remember when you were little and you were about to get punished for something you did and your parent would tell you to "come here," and you were afraid because you knew you were going to get the worst whipping ever? As children, you feel that the punishment would seem to last a lifetime. Not so! I have learned that if you just go ahead and go to your parent and take your punishment, the feeling won't last long, depending on how upset your parent is. It is the same way with our father in Heaven. He loves us unconditionally. He gave us many things starting with His son Jesus. Then He gave us two parents to love us unconditionally. Then He added other family members into the fold to love and look after us.

God is giving you an opportunity to come to Him so that He can care for you and protect you. What person in their right mind wouldn't want that? Okay, it takes a very long time to get to that point. God uses everyone for His purpose for your life. You have to find out what that purpose is. We all have dreams and goals. You can write these down and have them manifested. It could be anything you desire. When you come to Him in all sincerity, seeking His face and His kingdom, He will give you the desires of your heart. NO!!!! It doesn't happen overnight. It may take 10 years, or it may take 18 years. Remember this, though: you have to work in order to acquire your dreams and goals.

In all thy ways acknowledge Him and He will give you the desires of your heart. I desire a perfect relationship with Jesus that my finances will get better so that I can live comfortably. I desire a relationship with a God-fearing man, to be married, have children and travel. Even with travel, it takes a long time to get to where you want to go if you are going to a faraway place. God is simply stating: you read your Bible, but the scriptures point to Him and yet you still refuse to come to Him for the life He is trying to give you.

He wants you to live life more abundantly and the way to do that is to serve Him. We are not perfect, but He wants us to be; every day, there is a struggle with our flesh and spirit. There is warfare within ourselves and a majority of us may not get to where God wants us to be. However, He does need your help to help yourself to get where you want to be so that you won't continue to say you are not there yet. Where do you want to be?

CHAPTER 18

Throw Your Hands Up

Psalms 89:13: Powerful is your arm! Strong is your hand! Your right hand is lifted high in glorious strength.

November 13, 2013, my sister, her daughter, Kiana and I took a trip to Dallas, TX, when my niece was attending a workshop convention for dance. Okay, you are probably wondering, so what does that have to do with Psalms 89:13? It has everything to do with the scripture that I have chosen. My niece is not only a talented clogger, but she is also an extremely talented praise dancer as well. So, in her praise dancing, she usually has movements that require her to lift her hands high. I won't just be speaking about my niece lifting her hands high; in this chapter, I will speak on what causes people (including myself) to just throw up my hands.

On our way to Dallas, there was a song that came on the radio, and since my niece is a dancer, music is in her blood. She immediately threw her hands up and repeated what the performer sang in the song "Throw Your Hands Up." It's the same as what people my age used to say years ago, "just throw your hands in the air." In this day and time, the singers just shortened the term. When my niece sang along with the radio, a light bulb went off in my head, but as soon as I got home, I forgot what I was supposed to write about. So, here it is, several months later, working on this chapter.

As you can see, frustration can also cause someone's hands to just go up in the air to say, "I give up." There is no need to give up. Affirmations are good, but I once heard that instead of "affirmations," which is a statement that is declared to be true. Then if that be the case, then use the word this way: affirmation is things that are declared to be true that are made specifically for you.

It's not necessary to throw your hands up in frustration and give up on yourself or anyone else. Throw your hands up in praise because God did give you His only son, better days ahead and a life to live more abundantly. What better reason to lift your hands, shout and praise His Name.

I threw my hands up because of love. When you have been hurt so many times, there seems to be no hope in love. I am the type to fall in love quickly. I should know as well as anybody that love will come again. I have been told many times that I am worrying about the wrong things. The man who I thought was my Boaz ended up being married and constantly denying it when there was proof that he is. I won't say that all Nigerians are bad, and this man was just as beautiful as his heart "seemed" to be. He proposed to me in early 2014. This continued on and then all of a sudden, communication started slowing down. I would contact him and he wouldn't answer, but it would be two to three days later when he did answer.

A friend of mine said, "trust me, the man is seeing someone." Taking into consideration what my friend had told me, my heart continued to adore this man and hang onto his every word. Then, one day, after contacting him, he told me, "You are too inquisitive for my taste. You complain too much. I'm trying to concentrate at work. You don't expect me to talk to you every second." With my heart being hurt, I backed away for a bit. My friend once again told me, "check this man out." I told my friend several things that the man I love told me, and I believed him. I did more investigating, and to my surprise, as big as day on a well-known social media site, a picture of him and his wife in wedding attire cutting their wedding cake, posted June 2,

2014. Let me back up a minute...when he contacted me, his profile picture was of him and the beautiful young lady. I asked him about the picture and he told me that was he and his cousin attending a family wedding where the wedding party had to dress the same. But he put up another picture after I asked about the first photo with him and the same young lady who, this time, said she was his niece. Later, after confronting him, he pretended not to know the difference between a niece and a cousin. The first question he asked me was, "where did you get this picture?" I had explained to him that I hadn't lied to him like he had lied to me, stating that he wasn't on social media when in reality, he had been a member since March 30, 2009.

My heart immediately turned into an icebox and I threw my hands up. I stretched my hands to God, giving Him my icebox of a heart in hopes that He would chip away at this block of ice that I do call a heart and mend it.

CHAPTER 19

A Diva Moment

Esther 4:12: But the queen Vashti refused to come at the king's commandment by his chamberlains: THEREFORE, was the king very wroth, and his anger burned in him.

As you might be able to tell by now that Esther is one of my favorite books in the Bible and the story about a beauty pageant the king had put on to show how beautiful the women are. On this particular day, the king and soon-to-be queen held separate parties. Now, when I think about it and the Bible states "soon to be queen," that made it sound like they were not married, so these parties could have very well been what modernized people call a bachelor and bachelorette party, but nonetheless, it was set up to be a beauty pageant. When the king (Ahasuerus) called for his wife, she would not come into his presence, so she ended up being punished.

With Vashti not showing her face to the king and disrespecting him, his princes, and all the people in his province, she was punished for it; but before we talk about getting punished, let us have a look to why she didn't want to be in his presence. Mind you, both are having parties. Ahasuerus was drunk and maybe she was embarrassed, or maybe she was just having a good time. Did Vashti simply like not to be called? She just probably didn't want to come. When Vashti refused to show up, immediate action was taken.

Vashti had a "diva moment." Every female has a diva moment. A "diva moment" is a time when a female doesn't like what she has to do or feels that she can do it when she is good and ready. Esther 4 doesn't state the reason why Vashti refused to show up in his presence. All it states is that she refused to see what he wanted. We have all found ourselves not doing what other people asks us to do. I can't leave myself out. A diva moment can also be asking in a certain way the things that you desire to receive. In that case, men have their "diva moments," too. I crave for a diva moment and for a split second, I got it. At times I suppose, having "a moment" makes you feel important. Some people look at it as that person in their diva moment is snobbish and arrogant. I'm speaking on such things as when you go out to eat. Of course, you desire things to your liking so that you can be satisfied with what you eat, but the waiter or waitress may think otherwise.

I love having my diva moments because it makes me feel good. Is that wrong to feel that way? I guess you can be if you just don't get overboard with doing it. Then the people that work for you will not want to work for you any longer. At this point, I have no one working for me, so no diva momentsare brewing in my steam bath! A friend of mine purchased a beaded curtain that I've always wanted, so each time that I walk through that beaded curtain, it feels like I am the diva that I was born to be. It's all right to have your moments.

CHAPTER 20

What About Your Friends?

<u>Palms 41:9</u>: Yea, mine own familiar friend, in whom I trusted, which did eat of my bread, hath lifted up his heel against me.

We really need to be careful who we all call our friends. I had to learn the hard way, only to be hurt time and time again. Whether it's first-time meetings or you've known them for years. You have to really get to know them in order to trust them. They have to earn your trust. Why is it so difficult to do this? It could be the way we were brought up. The only people we were meant to trust is family, and even family nowadays isn't meant to be trusted; they could very well be your friend. When I think of family, I think of aunts, sisters, and cousins. Growing up, it would seem that I was sheltered, but as I got older, I realized that my parents {my grandmother and mother} taught me that family is important. All that I really dealt with was my aunt at home and then my sister. It was as if "we" were all we had. I could say that very well; these two were my friends. Outside the home, there were cousins with whom we associated within a school, church and maybe parties. Extracurricular activities took up most of the time that I wanted to spend with my sister and aunt. My aunt was in a band and my sister was in athletics. I tried both. I wanted to be in the band, but my mother told me that it took two hands to play an instrument. I wanted to play the trumpet, and what I visualized was me playing with one hand being the baddest ever marching on the football field. I made a 95 on my music test and that was the first instrument I chose that I wanted to play.

I was the second fastest in athletics tryouts, but I didn't have a way to get to practice. With the fact that I have Cerebral Palsy in volleyball, the way that I could serve at my best was not in the rules. I stayed in just to sit on the sidelines and work out. What good was that? But we are talking about friends. At an awkward age, every child feels as though they don't fit in. I was one of them. I kept to myself about feeling that way, smiled and pretended things were alright with me. Sure! I had friends and they were the greatest through elementary, jr. high and high school. I had switched friends when I first got to high school. My aunt told me that once I entered high school things would change and they did. There was nothing with my old friendships; it was just time to try new things and grow up. So, one day in study hall, my old friend came in, sat in front of me...not really knowing what was going on--nothing bad was said about each other; we just knew things were different. We talked until we cried together. After that, things were all right with us, and we spent as much time as we possibly could with each other. I enjoyed my new friends, though. Half of my friends spoke Spanish with me and had fun speaking it. The new friends I acquired were a grade ahead of me, so when they graduated, things changed dramatically for me. I felt lost. This new realm had me starting over again with making friends. I hated doing that. I really wasn't the same after that until a very old friend reentered into my life, and I found myself spending that time with him, which made me forget how difficult of a time I was having.

You never forget your friends. College is so totally different. College students are a unique brand of people even though you'll see them as the same people or they see themselves as the same as when they were leaving high school. But to me, college is another universe in itself. Different heights, weights, colors, views, identities, and morals...Aliens. You find yourself starting all over again as if you were in elementary. That's just me. Yes, I was glad to get away from home, but I didn't like the fact that I had to learn *PEOPLE* all over again. The attitudes were just astounding. College doesn't have to be a scary place. Did I ever find myself fitting in? No. I just played along to get through whatever shape, form or fashion I was turning into. I was known as "smiley" on campus. I would have to walk to my classes early in the morning and I found myself smiling. So, one morning, I was stopped by this gentleman who asked me, "Why are you smiling so early in the morning? Every time I see you, you're always smiling! I'm going to start calling you Smiley." I simply responded that it was just a beautiful day. The sun wasn't out so... He smiled, stating for me to keep on smiling and that it will make everyone else I run into smile. I thanked him for his kind words and he told me that he hoped to see me around. He was a very nice guy. Friends are hard to come by, even in your adult life, especially with social media. Everyone can be who they want to be behind a computer. I've come across several that I've had to just step back and watch the actions and I was calling them friends. A few turned out to be wolves in sheep's clothing. It's sad how you think that even if you have known them for at least three years, you still don't know them at all. They can get all the information needed and turn against you. Those are the ones that have nothing better to do with their lives and want to mess up your life because they are miserable. Who does that!? It's best to keep your old friends you grew up with. Even then, those friendships fall apart due to a misunderstanding, marriage, children or divorce. God didn't put you here on earth to deal with things alone, but God is the first one you should turn to when the ones you call friends have hurt you.

CHAPTER 21

I Am Not My Hair

<u>1 Corinthians 11:15</u>: But if a woman have long hair, it is a glory to her: for her hair is given her for a covering.

If to me is such a doubting word, so what "if" the woman *doesn't* have long hair? Then what? Every beautiful woman seems to be concerned about one thing. Can you guess what that one thing is? No, you may be thinking: relationships, work, children, self-worth. Yes, she may think about those things, including health. You could say that what they think about is considered as a part of health. Every morning when a woman wakes up and gets everyone else taken care of, she goes to the mirror and thinks, "what can I do with my hair today?" Depending on her profession, her hair can hang if it's long or put up in a bun. But for some of us, that is not the case. There may be some women who feel they can be more beautiful with longer tresses, but what if you don't have long tresses or it just simply won't grow and you've tried everything?

Purchase a wig? Get braids? Add extension? Whatever your decision, you are as beautiful as the day you were born with no hair. A video of a four-year-old girl was talking to her mother about a video she saw on her IPAD. The little girl kept saying the young man on the video wanted her to be happy and beautiful. Every day that you live, know that you are a gift. As the mother listened to the little girl explaining to her mother what the young man was saying, there was a caption in that video that the little girl suffered from hair loss called Alopecia after the loss of her grandmother and stress. This video went viral.

A few days later, I went to my dermatologist and I too was diagnosed with Alopecia. My heart sank. I thought of the little girl who had brought me to tears earlier in the week. I didn't know what to think. It frightened me because to me my hair makes me beautiful. Prior to finding out the news, I was taking care of my tresses with washing, conditioning, oiling my hair, eating right, drinking plenty of water and exercising. This isn't enough. Can you believe it? Supplements are good but can't take the place of proper nutrition. Stress, as mentioned earlier, is also the cause of Alopecia. This hair loss is said to occur in African American girls and women. This is caused by the pulling of hair having braids which can cause damage to the roots and destruction of the hair follicles. This is Traction Alopecia. Chemical Alopecia comes from using hot oil treatments and pomades that may cause inflammatory plugging to the hair follicles. Damage to the hair follicles will no longer grow hair. I have both diagnoses.

When I look back as a child, I realize that I've always had this problem and didn't know it. My hair would grow, come out, grow, come out, grow and come out. Several months ago, my hair was neck length; now, it's above my ears. All this time, I thought it was the medicine I was taking, but it wasn't. Instructions were given on the care of my scalp alone. I wash my hair with a shampoo that contains the ingredient Pyrithione Zinc which controls itching and dandruff, along with medicine that must be used twice a day for hair loss. I returned to my dermatologist in three weeks.

In the end, the best for healthy hair is natural hair. {No pun intended}

CHAPTER 22

Change Of Life

Matthew 9:20: And behold, a woman which was diseased with an issue of blood twelve years, came behind him, and touched the hem of his garment:

This will be the personal chapter out of all chapters because I am at that age where a woman's body changes. I was told by my family member that as you get older, your body changes. I was kind of prepared for it in my younger years. I don't sit back and pretend I am 20 or even 30. I'm grateful to have lived to the age I have. People can tell you what to expect as your body changes but not how to prepare for it.

The scripture may not actually deal with the change of life in women, but it was the closest word I could find when it was dealing with my issue. This is about it: the age of the woman was not given, but she has an issue. Her issue lasted 12 years; a women's issue lasts from the time she starts until it's time to "finish." Ladies, you all know what I'm talking about. The hot flashes, night sweats and mood swings. It's that relief when you come to a certain age and are told things will be changing for you. What does that mean? I've been this way since the day "it" started, so I don't know the difference.

When I was told, my heart sank. I didn't know how to handle it and have been waiting for this day and now that it's here...for days, I was in a blue funk about it. I've always wanted children and to know that my time for bearing a child has run out really hurts. Granted, there are plenty of children in this world who need a home, but I was told there is nothing like having one of your own. Still going through it and preparing for when it all stops. I am in the early stages. What comes along with the later stages of it? I believe it is supposed to be a happy time, a time to celebrate a new beginning of life. You've spent years spending money and to know you don't have to spend that much anymore is shocking. You're only spending $30.00 to $72.00 a year, depending on what brand is chosen and where.

When the woman with the issue of blood touched the hem of Jesus' garment, He knew He had been touched. To be told that you are all right because your faith has made you whole is shouting words. God's words are true. If we all just step out on faith, no matter what issue we may have, God can fix it.

CHAPTER 23

Sweet Dreams

<u>Matthew 11:28</u>: Come unto me, all ye that labour, and are heavy laden, and I will give you rest.

That sounds really good, doesn't it? It sure does! I don't labour {the spelling in the Bible} much, but there is a problem that I have to figure out the reason why I am not sleeping as I should. I never was one who could sleep well anyway, so growing up, being forced to go to sleep was difficult. Or let me put it in layman's terms: I was made to go to bed. I can understand it being a school night, but it was just hard. What happened was that I cried myself to sleep at night for as long as I could remember.

My favorite line from my parents was, "If you don't be quiet, I'm going to give you something to cry about." It was me, my sister and my aunt. When night came, I'd asked my aunt to sleep with me. I was a light sleeper then, so every move that was made, I woke up. She just really wanted to have a bed to herself, so the times she'd try to sneak out of bed, I'd ask her, "Where are you going?" She would slide right back into bed. I love her for putting up with me.

I started sleeping with a night light. Didn't really make anything better because now the light made it look like there were monsters on the wall. I continued to cry myself to sleep even with the night light on. I never shall forget the prayer I prayed at 13 about the night light:

Dear Heavenly Father, in the event that the lights should go out tonight, help me to not be afraid of the dark ~ Amen. How come it rained that night and the lights went out? I took a deep breath at bedtime and climbed into bed, and from then on, I actually stopped crying because I had found another way to get to sleep...I prayed. I found that praying myself to sleep was a way for me to become close to God without even realizing that I was doing that.

I have my own place and I sit up at night. Whenever I go to bed, I'm still praying for myself to sleep. The problem is that now, I can't get to sleep and I am up until five o'clock in the morning but find myself tossing and turning until close to seven o'clock in the morning. And I sleep all day. I really wish that I could find the root of this problem. I don't want to take any more medicine because I am already taking enough. This has been going on since October 2014, and I've tried to fix it on my own. Is that even possible? All things are possible through Jesus Christ. As I still pray, "all I want, God, is to get some rest." I go to Him in my distress. I can't seem to figure out what's going on in my world that I am worried about. Yes, I desire to have a relationship and there is no one around, but I don't see that as being the root of my problem. I was thinking about it constantly, but I always seem to find something that will occupy my time; then, it starts all over again the next day.

But what's really going on? I should be happy that I did receive the opportunity to love and be in relationships, but I've also wanted that relationship that would lead to marriage and people {sometimes family} just don't understand that. I've always wanted that for as long as I could understand what love and having a relationship was. My bottom line is: I want someone special in my life to share my success with. Some people choose to be single because let's face it! You don't have to worry about checking in with anybody; you can come and go as you please, you're only taking care of yourself and your needs and there is no arguing about it. What more could a person living the single life want? Singles says that it's all not peaches and cream. Those who say that are the ones who also desire a relationship.

I found that having someone in my life makes it easier for me to sleep at night. STOP THE PRESS!!!!!!!! I do have someone in my life. I have my family and my friends, but *they* don't live with me. So what made it hard for me to go to sleep growing up and I had family around me? Probably because I watched a few scary movies, but even before I started watching scary movies, I wanted someone next to me. I give all my heaviness to God or so; that's what I think that I am doing. When the prayer of desiring to be in a relationship got to the point I was tired of praying for it; I prayed for something else or for other people who are desiring the same things. There are those who already have their families, lost loved ones, and maybe don't have the desire to be with anyone else because they have lived their lives. I am not perfect and all I want to do is get some sleep.

I sometimes have to wonder that if I finally get into a relationship, will I want it? I had to turn my attention to something else. But every once in a while, the desire to want to be in a relationship creeps up on me. I'm going to continue to pray for my heart's desire because I am coming to Him for guidance and help. I know in the end, if it's not God's plan for me to be in a relationship or happily married, I pray that He will help me deal with, get through, and be satisfied with myself in being single.

CHAPTER 24

Best Relationship To Have

<u>Romans 5:11</u>: So now we can rejoice in our wonderful new relationship with God because our Lord Jesus Christ has made us friends of God.

I saw somewhere on a social network it said that the best relationship to ever have is with God. The only way to do that is through Jesus Christ because Jesus is God's son and God gave His son to save the world from our sins. So in return, Jesus sent a comforter to guide us in the time of need. Prayer is the decent and best way to have a relationship with God just because: Just because He wakes you up in the mornings, cradles you at night, and puts food on your table and clothes on your back. If you ask for it, He can also give you peace of mind when you absolutely need it. Reminds me of the song "God Will Fix It {After While}" A day for God is of a thousand years...AMAZING! So as long as I have lived, that is a very long time and everything comes easy for Him because He is God. Anything you need, He has it for you, but you must live right according to the word and believe in Jesus and His word for His word is true.

The only thing that gets me is having someone special in my life to share my success with. I wonder, at times, what am I doing wrong to have it where that man hasn't shown up? I keep hearing, "you are worried about the wrong thing." Is that so wrong to think about having that special one in my life when that is what I desire? First thing is first: I must seek God and the kingdom of Heaven. The second thing is that I must be so hidden in God that the man which God has chosen for me has to go through Him to find me. What's so hard about that? I'm not out in public actually showing myself off. I stop and think when it occurs to me that I have family and friends, but it's nothing like having that special someone in your life to share your day with. That's where God comes in. You will find that when you need or want someone to talk to, your friends are never around. That's a sign to let you know that God is there with an ear to listen. He truly is a friend indeed. He doesn't give answers right away, but He is there to listen day or night. All you have to do is call on Him and it is free of charge.

What people can't get a grasp of about me is what I always want is someone special to share my success with. This thought, this desire, keeps me up at night but not to the point I am saying that it is constant. When I am up, I do other things to occupy my mind and time. The thought is there, but it's vague. When I retire to my bed, I dread it because no one is physically there. People say that marriage isn't what it's cracked up to be ~ marriage is what you make it; I say that being single isn't what it's all cracked up to be, so I suppose being single is what you make it. You don't have to check in all the time, argue, or give side eyes wishing otherwise. I don't mind checking in or spending time. We all know space is needed.

It has gotten to the point that I don't know how to pray for my mate. How can you pray for a mate that doesn't exist or that you don't know about? It doesn't matter, you just pray. This is how you acquire a relationship with God. Don't just pray for what you want on your good days. Pray for others who may be sick, jobless, homeless, motherless, fatherless, childless, lonely or in prison. Always praise Him for what you do have, don't have, what He is going to do for you, and what He hasn't done for you yet; praise Him not only on your good days but also on your bad days. There may be a reason that He hasn't done the things your heart desires. He wants to make sure that you have Him first and you are real about your service to Him.

So, once again, the way to have a friendship with God is to pray.

CHAPTER 25

Chase The Bread

<u>Matthew 25:22</u>: He also that had received two talents came and said, Lord, thou deliveredst unto me two talents: behold, I have gained two other talents beside them.

Dedicated to Deuntae Hollins

I was trying to figure out what would be the next chapter in the book or the next phase of my life. I was having a conversation with a friend one night, discussing the economic situation that surrounds us every day. He was starting a new job and talking about how things were with his life and wanting to change a few things. The one main focus for him was to be able to make enough so that he could get things for his children. Most men want to be deadbeat dads, but this young man is willing to work for his just to get ahead. He was hoping that he would be able to work the weekend to get the extra money needed after his trial period of working.

Sitting on the sofa, these words came out of his mouth, "Gotta chase that bread." In figurative terms, bread meaning "dough," and dough meaning "money" right then and there, I had a revelation. I proceeded to tell him thank you and that he just broke my writer's block. A person never knows what can be turned into fruition unless you are to listen intensively. Money is not hard to come by. You have to go for what you know and just do it. It has been said that if you do what you love, you can make money from it. We all have many gifts and talents, but how far are we willing to hone those gifts and talents to get what we desire?

Some people work hard to make their dreams a reality and it may take years and then there are others with a natural gift or talent and get a spot right off. Growing up, some children know what they want out of life; some continue to play, be children and decide later what they want to do in life. It's always school, college, job, marriage and family, if at all that. Some grow up to be moguls. Example: Sean P. Diddy Combs. His life is like a dream come true when he had this idea that he wanted to work at a record company. He finagled his plan on what to do, how to do it, and when. He went on to become the largest producer and executive owner of his 'Bad Boy" label. I admire this man because he pushed for his dream and got the biggest rapper of all time off the street~the late Biggie Smalls. Sean Combs, in my eyes, did what no man could do...whether he knew it or not, he paid it forward. Even though we lost someone so young so soon, his music lives on.

What Sean did was take his gifts and multiplied them. He didn't hide his gifts or talents. He took what he had and helped the next man accomplish his dreams. The thing is, they started out small and became giants. The most profound words that were said were, "You can't change the world until you change yourself." That could be taken to mean a couple of things. Your world could be inside of you or the world of people itself, and that's exactly what they did.

What comes to mind where it seems at one point, Sean Combs said, don't chase the paper. I might have dreamed that. What it really means is to get up off your behind and go to work. Get a real job and stop hanging out in the streets all night, reminiscing on your youth. That life is over and it's time to grow up and take care of responsibilities. Some people come into their own extremely late because they are still trying to live in their hay days. How many of you have talents and gifts? Do you just wake up, straighten up and go to work? Do you like your job, or are you just doing something to pass the time? Find your niche, take steps in starting what you love and watch the bread chase you.

CHAPTER 26

Don't Take Any Wooden Nickels

Deuteronomy 11:16: Take heed to yourselves, that your heart be not deceived, and ye turn aside, and serve other gods, and worship them.

This particular chapter deals specifically with the heart as in other chapters. We walk around in this life believing what other people tell us when it comes to having or wanting a relationship, or we fall into that emotional realm in thinking that someone cares about you when they are just actually out to serve themselves and their desires. I tend to overlook the bad in people because I feel like there is some good deep down inside of them.

Many years before my friend passed, and way before I knew he was sick, we had a conversation. He rightly apologized for treating me the way he did and said that he wanted to see me happy even if it wasn't with him. The breakup was horrifying, yet, I finally forgave him after forgiving myself. It took a while to do so because there were words exchanged that didn't need to be exchanged all because of misunderstanding. The conversation was a gentle and memorable one. My friend met the man whom I started to have a relationship with. In my friend's eyes, I seemed happy and he was happy for me. We spent the day together at the movies and had dinner.

We enjoyed that time together, laughing and carrying on. Little did I know how sick he really was. He said, "You seem happy. Is he treating you good?" If you don't ever remember anything else I tell you, remember this, don't take any wooden nickels. You deserve the best." He mentioned this to me again after finding out how sick he was and I went to see him in the hospital. The nurse said, "You have a visitor. Wake up to see who it is." He smiled that gorgeous smile that always brightened my day. I asked if he knew who it was? And he shook his head, saying my name the only way he could say it. He proceeded to tell me how he ended up in the hospital, how he was just ready to go home and wanted me to come with him and take care of him. I was flattered and didn't know how to respond to that. But before I answered, he remembered that I was with someone and wanted to make sure that it was okay with the new man in my life. We shared a laugh and I told him that I would return to see him.

That evening he was transported to another hospital because he had gotten worse. I didn't know until later when his niece called me crying, saying that he wasn't waking up. I couldn't get myself together quick enough to hold it together. I let loose for 20 minutes. I just couldn't stop crying. I thought that taking a shower would help, but it didn't, so I just had to go through it. All I could think about was what if I had said "yes" to this man who wanted to marry me? Would he still be living today? It just seemed as though it was my fault, but he broke up with me. That was on my mind and I couldn't fight that question. The answer came like a flash of light. "You can't save someone's life by being with them. Sickness falls on everyone. Everyone has to leave this earth. It was his time." That was a hard pill to swallow.

I made it to see him twice. The first time was with his niece. He didn't respond to me and it seemed as though he was angry with me. It was just my imagination. I'm glad he heard me though. I told him that I would return and I did the next evening. I ran into his nieces on the way in and they had tears in their eyes. His oldest niece said, "He didn't respond to us, maybe he will respond to you." I hugged her and said my goodbyes. I went in to see him. I wanted him to get up out of that bed so badly and just live. I held his hand and wiped his forehead. He knew I was there as if he was waiting for me to show. I didn't want to leave. He seemed to respond to me this time. I said that it seemed as though he knew I was there because four hours later, he passed away. Sometime after the funeral, he came to me three nights in a row playing with me and reminding me not to take any wooden nickels.

He has been gone for a few years now and in between that time, I have loved and lost. Or just loved and not having another relationship. Not because of him but because being found by a decent man isn't happening for me. I have dated, but the men that I've dated and liked are emotionally unavailable. This in itself is hurtful. But my Father understands my pain. What I'm doing my best to do is stay focused and do what He will have me to do because He knows my future and He will not bring any harm to me but give me hope and a future. I have to believe that and hold on to it.

In the meantime, there is someone that I really like, but I don't know how to express myself enough to sit down and have that talk with him. I do believe that he, too is emotionally unavailable. He said some things that made me feel as though it is not me he is looking to be with. It would be nice to be with him, showing him how an earthly king is supposed to be treated, but I chose not to stand in God's way of Him doing His job in working on this man's heart for me. I asked that of Him and in the end, the man that I care about might just be that wooden nickel that I don't need in my life.

CHAPTER 27

Mama's Baby, Father's Maybe {Sperm Donor}

<u>Job 19:15</u>: They that dwell in mine house, and my maids, count me for a stranger; I am an alien in their sight.

I don't want to repeat myself, but I may have touched on this a bit. A while back, I was trying to get my father's number. Come to find out, he feels that the only time that I call is when I want money. This information hurt me when I read those words. When I say read, I mean that the message was sent to me through social media. These are totally false accusations. I communicated with him without having to ask him for anything; then, one day he offered, I accepted and waited. When that day never came, then I would ask. I'm not one to pick up the phone and really call anyone. This lets me know that he doesn't want me to have his number.

Why should I worry and make myself sick over a man who meant me no good anyway? He'd come around so that I could go visit with my grandmother and the rest of the family; {his mother}. I enjoyed my time with her and my cousins. Little did I know, they really didn't want me around. I was young and all you want is love from your family at that age. I suppose I looked over what they thought and did my best to fit in. I think I stopped going around that family when I became a teenager. I missed my aunts and cousins and tried to remain in touch, but as you know, when you get older, you lose touch with many things as life becomes busy.

In my college years, I ran across one of my cousins and it was extremely good to see her. She seemed to do her best to avoid me as if she was better than I was. So, I quickly caught on to that and just smiled in passing. I love her and my cousins from a distance and still do my best to keep in touch with them. I was in and out of college so let me back up a few years. My mother and I went to court because after so many years, she was finally getting her divorce. This is how I see it: Father left when I was a child and didn't return for good until I was 18. Doesn't make sense right?! If he was having me to spend time with family? So, I'll say he left in my early teens. When the question was asked, "In this union, there was born a child?" His response: "They say..." What child wants to hear the man that is supposed to be in his or her life say that? I LOOK JUST LIKE THAT MAN!!!!

I was about 21 years old then. Here's the kicker! Years later, he comes around town telling my other relatives that I'm not his child. This was some time after his mother had passed away {R.I.L. Grandma Ophelia}. So, I gave this man I call father a call. His wife at the time would not take him the phone, but I insisted that she take him the phone so that I could speak with him. After so long, he gets on the phone. I gave him a piece of my mind and he denied that he ever said anything about me not being his child. He continued to say that I wasn't thereafter. So, I prayed on it, forgave myself and forgave him. Did it do any good? No. I spent time with him trying to make amends and become closer to him; yet, all he could do was throw his other children in my face stating that he has grandchildren from a woman he raised that doesn't belong to him to whom he is claiming. But he can't claim me--okay.

Every female wants that father figure in her life to show her what a real man is unless he's the type to abuse his spouse and that's all the young girl sees and feels like that's the way she is supposed to be treated. I wanted that love from my father, but he'd talk in his third-person voice which had no feeling.

"Daddy loves you," he would say. He wasn't a personal man at all. He came down a few times and I thought we were getting somewhere. During the time he denied me, he was claiming 17 other children but asked me to come take care of him for a week when he got sick. This request boiled my blood so, I told him, "I can barely take care of myself. Why don't you get the other 17 kids you are claiming to take care of you because I can't do it." You may ask: can't or won't? Maybe both. But I'm not going to subject myself to being mistreated when he feels that I'm not his daughter. He's showing me that he doesn't want anything to do with me by not giving me his number.

There were deaths in the family and all I wanted to do was check on him to see if he was all right. He can now say what he wants to because he doesn't ever have to worry about me being a part of his life as his daughter again. But I have a Heavenly Father and Daddy who has carried me throughout my childhood, sending me a vessel as beautiful as my mother and she has been both to me.

Any man can make a baby, but it takes a real man to be a dad.

***Since the writing of this chapter, my father passed away on August 7, 2015; R.I.L. ***

CHAPTER 28

I'm Not About To Play With You

Genesis 11: 8-9: So the Lord scattered them from there over all the earth, and they stopped building the city. 9 That is why it is called Babel----because the Lord confused the languages of the whole world. From there the Lord scattered them over the face of the whole earth.

Dedicated to Janice Rene Daniels and ZaKelya Jefferson

When God told the families of the son of Abraham to move, they didn't so, God took it upon Himself to move them and then made it so that no one would understand each other because at first, the languages were the same. This makes me think about the different cultures that are in the world and all types of dialect there is and some are understood and some are not. This is not about understanding languages, it's about obeying God and the consequences we all face when we don't adhere to God's word. I will tell anyone that I am nowhere near perfect, but I do my best to be because that's what God wants.

No matter what we go through in life, we are responsible for what we do and say to each other and to ourselves. Have you just ever sat back and wondered why you haven't gotten as far as you want to go in life with your goals? It's because of your mindset and how you feel about yourself and others. And also how you treat yourself and others. There are many incidents in the Bible where God tells His children to do something and sometimes they did obey and other times they didn't. When the children got into trouble, they called out to God and once again, He saved them from whatever destruction they caused themselves to be in, and then they would go right back to doing what they would be doing and then get caught up in the same situation ~ only to turn around again and pray to get out of it. The same is as of today for those who know God for themselves. We are given freedom to the point that we should obey God's commandments. Do we? I haven't met one who has, not even me. I believe I have mentioned before that I will tell someone with a quickness that I'm not perfect and no one is. I am definitely no exception. Just like God's children in Israel and Egypt, God grew tired of the same thing over and over again when His "babies" kept sinning--just like He grows tired of us saying that we will change *"if You only just get us out of this predicament this time."* Do we? Sometimes.

As long as we live and have this fleshly body, we will continue to sin *unless* we have that strength not to. That strength can only come from God. When you continue to act up, you will get punished one way or another, or God will send you a message by using other people for you to get the **"hint."**

CHAPTER 29

Three Of Me

<u>2 Corinthians 5:8</u>: **We are confident, I say, and willing rather to be absent from the body, and to be present with the Lord.**

Dedicated to Sheila Crawford and Raymond Hayes

For many years, I've had partial seizures; the doctors didn't know what they were and would not call it epilepsy. The first ever was in fifth grade. It seems to always happen at the time I am eating or after I eat. I was in the cafeteria with my friends. We had all sat down in our spot facing the wall, said grace and began to eat. I opened my milk and took a drink. I figured I swallowed too hard because after that my stomach and throat hurt. Next thing I know, one of the teachers who was the smallest thing in school was picking me up off the floor. I guess no one would go near me. After I came to, the word had gotten outside of the cafeteria that I had passed out. I noticed my friends standing off, crying and scared. I was taken to the office and to the nurse to see if I had a concussion. I hit my head on the corner of the lunch table as my friend told me when I called her that afternoon to find out what happened. She said that she and my other friends thought I was playing. Some joke, right?

My mother came to pick me up and took me to the doctor and it turned out to be strep throat. I stayed home for the rest of the day. That was the day of the play my English class was supposed to do "Pacos Bill." I received a 0 as a grade because I wasn't there. I tried to explain to my teacher that what happened couldn't be helped. As a student knows, it takes four 100's to bring a grade up. I begged for extra work to do so that I could do my best to get that 0 off my grade book, but I had to wait for work and did my best to make 100 on the next four papers. The next day at school, people were asking questions to what happened; some things I could not answer and my friends were heroines to me because they seemed to have my back and protected me from things that I wasn't ready for {Thank you Elisa Black Sims, Paige Sanders, Esther Forte ~ the awesome threesome.} That was 1979 or 1980, and Reagan was president.

It is amazing what your brain can remember and what it can't. The next "episode" was in February 1995; my grandmother had to see about me. I had this nasty habit of locking the bathroom door. My grandmother heard a loud thump, went to the bathroom and I managed to unlock the door. Obviously, I didn't know what happened and my grandmother seen it and she said she was talking to me, *"Don't you leave me."* She went to get my mother and I was still sitting on the toilet...mother comes in asking, "What's wrong with you?" I told her that I didn't know, "I think I passed out." I don't remember what happened that night but I do remember my mother taking me to the doctor the next day. I had a minor concussion. The doctor stated that if I had hit my head closer to my eye, I would have lost it.

The next seizure happened a year later. My grandmother started keeping up with them. I figured that I was working out too much and I had lost 11 pounds in two weeks. This happened again during the day and my sister was in college. Our cousin, who was a nurse, came over to check me out and said that my colon was cutting up. The doctors still couldn't find out what was wrong. I still needed to be watched. Once again, it happened a year later, in the summer of 1997. My sister and aunt happened to be home. I was sitting up with my aunt until she finished a paper she was working on for

Sunday because she was speaking. So, that would let you know that the incident happened Saturday night. I told my aunt that my stomach was hurting and I'm going to the bathroom. From the second time it happened, I knew not to lock the door. My aunt followed me into the bathroom and that's when something new happened. I seen what was going on. My aunt was cradling my head in her arms, telling me things will be alright and to come back to them. I felt something cold on my head. I saw my sister crying, but I couldn't say anything. I was floating over a set of colorful trees, not wanting to come down. For some reason, I smelled food. It felt so good, I really didn't want to come down. When I was myself, I asked my sister why was she crying? My mother had come and probably was really hurt seeing me that way.

May 2000 was an early morning. This pain woke me up. I made it to my sister's room where my aunt was sleeping and I had kneeled down by then and told my aunt that I wasn't feeling well. Next thing, my grandmother called my name. My aunt said she took off running {laughing out loud.} Nothing is funny about the situation, but thinking about how my aunt would just take off is funny. That was the year I took a trip with my father to Minneapolis, Minnesota. My family felt that taking trips wasn't for me and that the seizures were stress-related.

It doesn't stop there. Seven years would pass and in the month of May, the fainting spells also happened again. I seen myself this time walking within the same set of trees, but they were burnt and I was walking on the ashes of the trees. That was early Wednesday morning, around 2 a.m. I came to and thought, *"Oh no, I passed out again."* I made it back to the bed and it was so cold. When I rested and woke up later, I had to tell my mother because I had this sick look on my face. My grandmother was at the table eating. She was hurt that I didn't tell her. I didn't want to disturb her sleep. Mother took me to the doctor to find out what was going on. The doctor asked me everything right down to what type was the moon? It went from a dumping sensation to asthma and my Cerebral Palsy that was causing the episodes. Met with a neurologist and had test run and the doctor told me that my brain was extremely active and it would cause seizures and he put me on this certain medicine that actually caused hallucinations and thoughts of suicide. I stopped taking them.

Then four years later, once again, it happened. By now, you would think, I'm so tired of this ~ me and my body. I had come home from school and it had been a rough day. That night, I was on the phone with my ex and he said he was just calling my name several times. I know I didn't doze off. With that, I cut the conversation short and said good night.

2015 March, I was hanging out with my friend. I had purchased Blue Bell Butter Crunch and we went to her apartment. It had been a minute since I had seen her, so she stopped by and scooped me up. As we sat at the table catching up on things, laughing and enjoying each other's company, my ears started ringing and then I couldn't hear anything. I told her that my stomach was hurting and we were still both cracking up. I remember her asking me if I was all right? At that point, I could feel myself thinking she is going to tell you that you are going to have a seizure. By then, I felt myself leaving my body. I also told her that I need to lay down, but she wouldn't let me lay down because if I had gotten up, I would have bumped my head. Then the strangest thing happened. Mind you, this has happened twice before, but not like this.

I saw myself at the top of the ceiling, floating above me and my friend, wearing what looked like a white gown. It could have been a glowing light surrounding me; all I know, it was white. I heard her thoughts. She was trying to calm herself down and the other side of her was arguing with her calm self, yet, she wasn't talking. The "other" me was sitting in the chair, facing the chair she was sitting in, but the "other" me saw us still laughing. The third me was standing by my right shoulder. I remember telling her that I didn't want to come down. I tried to eat what she had given me, but it was too sweet. She said, *"Stacey, you are about to have a seizure."* When I was coherent, or so I thought, she said, *"Stacey, you had a seizure."* She said I looked at her and said, "Oh no! really?! Oh My God. How is he?" It confused her. In my mind, I was thinking she was still talking about her ex and cracking jokes. I know she kept asking me if I was all right and what was her name? She said I was looking at her weird and laughing and told her who she was. *"Yes, I know who you are...Sheila"* I didn't mean to scare her. She kept talking to me...I made it to the sofa because she helped me. I remember taking off my shoes. She continued to talk to me until she felt that I was myself. I really don't think that I was myself because half the things didn't make sense. She was still asking if I was all right. And the sweetest thing she did was continue to crack jokes.

I told my male friend from Wilmington, Delaware about the crossover and he helped me to understand different things. Even though I understood what happened, he was intrigued by it happening to me. He constantly texted me the whole time he was at work. He stated that we are three parts: Spirit, soul and body. We are spiritual beings. We possess a soul and then we are held here by a physical body. We are not of this world, a creature created by He who created existence in God's likeness. We are a spirit that is our former body. The soul is our life...like a physical body needs blood, a spirit needs a soul. When we die, we don't die; we move on. He said that by telling him what happened to me, I blessed him; I freed him from the fear of death.

But I will often wonder what the reason was for the three of me this time.

CHAPTER 30

A Purpose Driven Life

<u>Jeremiah 29:11</u>: "For I know the plans I have for you," declares the Lord, "the plans to prosper you and not to harm you, plans to give you hope and a future.

God was speaking through Jeremiah in a letter to the surviving elders of Jerusalem. This is good news! For so many years, the children of Israel were in exile and now it was time for them to be freed. All the children had to do was seek God first and not believe the lies that were told to them. In this day and time, we can find ourselves in exile because of the situations we put ourselves through. When we find that we can't handle certain situations, we hide ourselves from the world until we think that it's safe to show our faces when things get better for us. But in reality, things won't get better until we seek God first sincerely.

As a child growing up, we find ourselves under the protection of our parents and we won't have to want for anything as long as we feel protected. We are all God's children no matter how bad we are; He still shows us mercy. That's enough to give Him praise because He is that kind of God. What kind of protection are you looking for? Or what kind of future are you hoping for? You think insurance companies have you covered completely? In the end, you still have to pay a high cost for coverage. Well, your family does when all God asks you to do is serve Him and He will give you the desires of your heart, love, comfort AND full protection from dangers seen and unseen.

God has a plan for you the moment you are born ~ you just don't know it. Throughout life, you may be given a series of tests to see how well you can cope. You may not fully understand it until you reach a certain age, but the knowledge is there. Your eyes are called the "looking glass," so who you see as a child can be etched into your brain as you get older. People come and go. Things, places, and possibly tastes become memories. As you get older, you reminisce about the good old days and do your best to forget the bad ones.

I wanted to be many things growing up. A firewoman, A private detective, a tennis player, a gymnast, a singer, an actress, a television anchorwoman working alongside Tom Brokaw and a DJ. All these things that I was willing to try in order to be the "best me" that I could be, but God had something different in mind. I majored in Communications, but I found myself loving English in high school, so I had to make a choice. I believed in myself enough to know that I could get somewhere with either one of these subjects, but it had to take God to push me further to that goal. I majored in it, but I didn't graduate from it, but God still had a plan. So much so that all the things that I learned, I put to good use and started networking. Back to English, I love to write and do research. During a semester in English, we studied Literature which is the entire body of writings of specific languages, periods and people: including essays, poetry, novels, history and biography. We learned 18th-century poetry and that's when I really fell in love with poetry.

Taking all that I've learned up to college, after college and surrounding myself in the school system when a person looks at my resume,' everything falls back into my major and writing. So, even though I couldn't see it, God has a plan for my future because I prayed. One of my prayers was that I wanted to be famous, but I just didn't know how that was going to happen. I continued to do what I loved the most...write/poetry. I also love beautiful hands, so I also majored in Cosmetology for doing nails. I would say that I am a true **"Poetic Justice."** God wants everyone to have a future. My break came when I was asked to write a piece for the American Cancer Society when my sister worked for them. It was an honor. It was for the volunteers for a race that was being done. Things just took off from there. My sister encouraged me to do something with it, and doors were finally opened; small, but yet, they opened. I began to write poetry and keep them around. A few pieces I wish I could get back. My mother invested in me. She purchased me a Brother typewriter. I loved that. Years later, I advanced to a computer that my late cousin, Roland Harris, purchased for me, and I promised to keep up the work on it when it started giving me problems. The computer lasted me all of a good 13 years of service. In between that time, I wrote letters, sent manuscripts, waited and continued to write. Then, I started networking and word got around; I started getting invitations to church services to do my pieces for certain themes. With the help of a local author, he put me on the right path to where I needed to go and for his help, I supported him in his writings.

God placed me with people whom He felt that I needed to get to know, become friends with and learn from them. My first book of poetry was published and released by my 35th birthday. That was 2004. My family had thrown me the biggest party ever {or what seemed to be the biggest party ever} I continued to write, and a different company published and released my second book in 2012. It's difficult to keep up with what I'm doing now, but I'm still writing.

I have yet to see where I am headed, but God has a bigger master plan in store for me as He does for all of you. All you have to do is ask Him and believe that He will do what He said He will.

GOD'S MASTER PLAN
ABOUT THE AUTHOR

Stacey Barlow

Stacey was born in Texarkana and raised in Hooks, TX. She is a three times Editors' Choice Award winner, a graduate of Hooks High School, Texarkana College, Longridge Writers Group {home study}, and C'C's Cosmetology College. A resident of Texarkana, TX, Stacey continues to pursue her dream in writing with other projects in the near future. Stacey is a former online radio personality looking to revamp her show, Limitless and calling it: Limitless: Coffee Break. She is also one of Amazon's # 1 Best-Selling authors through her contribution to "How Big Can You Dream?" and an online counselor for the Crisis Text Line.

She has published previous books: "Cold Hearted Warm Hearted," "Rejuvenation: Innocent Until Proven Guilty," "Precious Jewels," and "A Taste of Honie."